STAIRWAY TO TERROR

I could dimly see, by the distant street lights, that the curtain at the window was blowing out, and flapping in the wind.

Out, and not in! That took a moment to register in my mind, and then it meant only one thing. Someone somewhere in the house had opened either an outside door or a window.

Just then something fell in the hall, or rather on the stairs to the third floor.

I had an irresistible impulse to crawl into bed beside Miss Juliet and cover my head with the bedclothes. But as the old stairs creaked one after another, there was no room for doubt.

Someone was stealthily climbing the stairs to the third floor.

The next second I was out in the dark hall and feeling my way to the locked door to the back flat. I wanted Hugo; I wanted Hugo and Mary. I wanted somebody near, and the fact that, in spite of everything, I still suspected Hugo of the murder seemed at that minute to have no importance whatsoever.

In a condition approaching panic I groped my way through that awful darkness, and flung myself against the door. "Hugo!" I called. "Hugo!"

Suddenly I was falling, and that is all I remember.

When I came to, I was lying flat on my back. Mary, in her nightgown was sprinkling water on my face. "You fainted," she said shortly.

But I knew that I most certainly had not fainted . . .

MISS PINKERTON

Mary Roberts Rinehart

Garden City, New York

CHAPTER I

It seemed to me that I had just gone to bed that Monday night when I heard the telephone ringing and had to crawl out again. When I looked at my watch, however, I saw that it was a few minutes after one. A trained nurse grows accustomed to such things, of course; but I had set that particular night apart to catch up with my sleeping, and I was rather peevish when I picked up the receiver.

"Hello."

"This Miss Adams? Inspector Patton speaking."

He did not need to tell me that. I had had a sort of premonition when the bell rang that the police had turned up another case for me, and I wanted one that night about as much as I wanted hardening of the arteries. In fact, I said as much.

"Listen to me, Inspector. I need some sleep. I'm no good the way I am."

"Then you're not on a case now?" He knew that I often took what we call eighteen-hour duty, and slept at home.

"I'm still resting from that last one," I said rather sharply, and I imagine he smiled. He knew well

5

enough what I was talking about. I had been taking care of a gangster's wife for him in order to get a line on who came to the house. But the gentleman in question kept his business and his family too well separated, and besides, she was the most jealous woman I ever saw—and a trained nurse sees a lot of them. I am pretty much given to minding my own business when I am on a case, especially when it is a police case; but the moment any female in a white cap and a uniform enters certain houses, there is sure to be trouble.

"This is different," he said, "and it may be for only a few hours. Better call a taxi and come over. Do you know the Mitchell house on Sylvan Avenue?"

"Everybody knows it. What's wrong?"

"I'll tell you when you get there. I'm at the drugstore on the corner. How long will you be?"

"About a half hour," I said. "I *had* hoped to get some sleep tonight, Inspector."

"So had I!" he retorted, rather testily for him, and hung up the receiver.

That was a Monday night, the fourteenth of September. If they ever have to perform an autopsy on me, they will not find Calais written across my heart, but that date.

I drew a long breath; looked at my bed; at the uniform which needed buttons, draped over a chair, and my sewing basket beside it; and then I looked through the door into my little sitting room, newly done in chintz, and at my canary, snugly covered in his cage so that he would not burst into song at dawn and rouse me. Rouse me!

I can write that and fairly weep. Rouse me! When

6

for that night and the next four nights sleep was to be as rare with me as watercress in the Sahara. Rouse me! When just four nights later it was to look as though nothing but Gabriel's horn would ever waken me again.

Well, I am not as bitter as I sound, and that night I was merely resigned. I got down and dragged my suitcase from under my bed, threw in a few toilet articles—for it is always packed and ready—called a taxi and then got into a uniform. But I was not excited or even greatly interested. Indeed, at the last minute, finding in my suitcase a snub-nosed little automatic which the Inspector had given me, I picked it up gingerly and looked around for a place in which to hide it. It would never do for Mrs. Merwin, my landlady, to find it; so I finally decided to put it in the jardinière with my Boston fern. She never remembered to water that fern anyhow.

I suppose that is funny when I look back over it. But it is not really funny at all. Later on I planned to go back one day and get it; but it would never have done me any good, as I know now. And, as I think back over those particular five days, I realize that on the only occasion when I might possibly have used it, I was fighting madly to get air into my lungs. All I could think of was that, to get air, to breath again. Well . . .

So I was not in the best of humor that night when I closed my suitcase and pinned on my cap. To tell the truth, I was wondering why I continued my work for the police. One way and another I had run a good many risks for them and lost a lot of sleep. I felt that I committed no breach of faith in using my profession

7

as a cloak for other activities. I had never neglected a patient for them, and I had used hours when I needed rest to help solve some piece of wickedness or other. I knew I had been useful. Pretty nearly every crime from robbery up to murder leads to a call for a doctor, and often enough for a nurse, too. As for professional ethics, I have never known of criminals who had any, even among themselves. It has been my experience that there is no honor among thieves.

But what had I got out of it myself, except the doubtful reward of being called Miss Pinkerton when the Inspector was in a good humor? There were a good many days, and nights, too, when I sighed for the old peaceful days. Taking special duty at the hospital, and at seven or seven thirty the night nurse coming in and smiling at the patient.

"How's Miss Adams been treating you today? Holding out on food as usual?"

Wandering out into the hall with her, exchanging notes on the case and a bit of hospital gossip, and then going home. The night air cool and fresh after the hospital odors, Dick hopping about in his cage, and nothing to do until the next day.

"Sugar, Dick?"

Getting the sugar, while he watched me with eyes like small jet beads; watering the fern; Mrs. Merwin coming in at nine o'clock with a glass of hot milk and a cookie.

"It will make you sleep, dearie."

And then I had made the alliance with Inspector Patton and the Homicide Squad. By accident, but they had found me useful from the start. There is one thing about a trained nurse in a household: she can

8

move about day and night and not be questioned. The fact is that the people in a house are inclined pretty much to forget that she is there. She has only one job, ostensibly, and that is her patient. Outside of that job she is more or less a machine to them. They see that she is fed, and, if she is firm, that she gets her hours off-duty. But they never think of her as a reasoning human being, seeing a great deal more than they imagine, and sometimes using what she sees, as I did.

With the patients, of course, it is different. They are apt to consider her as something halfway between a necessary nuisance and a confessor. Most of the time the nuisance, but take a sleepless night, with everything quiet, and about three in the morning they begin to talk. I have listened to some hair-raising confessions in my time. Sometimes these confessions had to go to Headquarters, but most of the time they did not. The police were not interested in evasions of the moral law. They were only bored with unfaithful husbands and wives, and evasions of income taxes, and what not. And to the Homicide Bureau, of course, there was only one crime. That was murder.

My exact relation to the Bureau has never been defined. One day a police captain referred to me as a "stool," by which he meant stool pigeon. I have seldom seen the Inspector so angry.

"Stool!" he said. "What the devil do you mean by that, Burke? Miss Adams is a part of this organization, and a damned important part. We've got a lot of wall-eyed pikes around here calling themselves detectives who could take lessons from her and maybe learn something."

Sometimes, as I say, he called me Miss Pinkerton, but that was a joke between us. I have never claimed to be a detective. What I had was eyes to use and the chance to use them where the police could not.

But I did not want to use them that Monday night. I wanted to shut them for eleven hours or so, and then go out the next day and do some shopping. I am ashamed to think of the bang with which I closed my bag, or of the resentment with which I lugged it down to the front door. No use letting the taxi driver ring the bell and waken everybody.

I felt better in the night air, and in the taxi I tried to put my mind on whatever work lay ahead. I had gathered from the Inspector's voice that something grave had happened, and I reviewed what I knew of the family. There were only two of them, old Miss Juliet herself and her nephew, a good-looking weak-chinned boy. He was her sister's child, and that sister had married, late in life, a man who was no good whatever. There was a story that he had squandered her money and then Miss Juliet's, but I am not sure of that. Anyhow, they had both died long ago, and the old lady was certainly impoverished and had the boy into the bargain.

I hear a good bit as I go around. In a city the size of ours, big as it is, there are always one or two dominating families, and for many years the Mitchells had been among them. So I had heard about the old lady and this boy, and I knew that she had had her own troubles with him. For years she had kept him away, at school and college, but he did no good at either, and he had been at home for some months now, sometimes working at whatever offered, but mostly loafing. His name was Wynne, Herbert Wynne, and he must have been twenty-four or thereabouts

It was known that they got along badly, and what I anticipated that night, as the taxi turned into the neglected grounds behind their high iron fence, was that some trouble had developed between the two of them. To tell the truth, I had an idea that the boy had turned on Miss Juliet in some frenzy of anger, and possibly injured her. And I was not surprised, as the taxicab turned into the Mitchell place between old iron gates, which had never been closed within my recollection, to find that the house, usually dark, was lighted from roof to cellar.

What I had not anticipated was that, within a few feet of the entrance, the car should come to a grinding stop, and that the driver's voice should be lifted in wrath and alarm.

"Get out of there! Do you want to be killed?"

I looked out of the window, and I could see a girl in the roadway, just ahead of us.

"Please, just a minute!" she said, in a breathless sort of voice. "I must speak to whoever is in the car."

"What is it?" I called.

She came straight toward me, and by the light of a street lamp I could see her clearly, a pretty little thing, about twenty perhaps, in a light coat and a beret, and with a face so pale and shocked that it fairly made me gasp.

"What's wrong in there?" she demanded, still breathlessly. "Is somebody hurt?"

"I don't know. I imagine somebody is ill. I'm

11

a nurse."

"Ill? Then why is there a police car at the door?"

"Is there one? I really don't know. Why don't you ask? It looks as though there are people in the hall."

She stepped back a foot or two and stood staring at the house. "They wouldn't want a nurse if anyone was—if anyone was dead," she said, apparently thinking out loud. "It might be a robbery, don't you think? If they heard someone in the house, you know."

"It's possible. Come up with me, and we'll find out."

But she drew back. "Thanks, but I'll run along. They didn't say what it was, when they sent for you?"

"Not a word."

She seemed reluctant to let me go. She stood beside the window of the taxi, holding onto it and staring at the house. Then it seemed to occur to her that what she was doing required some explanation, and she turned to me again.

"I was just passing, and when I saw all the lights and that car—I suppose it's really nothing. I just— would it be all right for me to telephone you a little later? If it would bother you, or you'd be asleep. . . ."

I looked at the house, and the police car standing in front of it, and I imagine my voice was rather grim when I answered her.

"From the look of things I'll not be getting much sleep," I said. "But you'd better give me your name, so I can leave word to be called."

It seemed to me that she hesitated. "That doesn't matter, does it? I'll call you, and you'll know who it is."

With that she left me, and I saw her going out the gate. I had seen a small coupé standing some distance off, before we turned in, and I felt certain that it belonged to her. But I forgot her almost immediately, as the taxi got under way again with a jerk that almost broke my neck.

Before me lay the old house, blazing with lights. Always I had been curious about it; now I was to know it well. To know the way it creaked and groaned at night; to see revealed in broad daylight its shabby gentility, its worn remainders of past splendors, and to hear my own voice at night echoing through its rooms while I shouted at the deaf old woman in her bed, "Can I get you anything, Miss Juliet?" Or, "Are you more comfortable now?"

For Miss Juliet was safe enough, lying there in her wide old walnut bed with her reading glasses and her worn Bible on the table beside her. Safe enough; that night at least.

I can write all this comfortably now, filling in the hours while I wait for one of those cases in which I start with one patient and end with two. Every time I take such a case, I contemplate a certain suggestion made by the Inspector at the end of the Mitchell tragedy, and I turn it over in my mind.

But in the interval I am writing the story of that tragedy, the stork—a bird which I detest anyhow—is a trifle late as usual, and so I have plenty of time. For a good many months, however, I could not even think about the Mitchell case, or the Mitchell house, or old Miss Juliet Mitchell lying there in her bed.

CHAPTER II

There were three or four men in the hall when the taxi stopped, and one of them, a Doctor Stewart, whom I knew by sight, came out onto the porch to meet me.

"It's Miss Adams, isn't it?"

"Yes, doctor."

"Your patient is upstairs, in the large front room. The cook is with her, and I'll be up at once. I've given her a hypodermic, and she ought to get quiet soon."

"She has had a shock, then?"

He lowered his voice. "Her nephew committed suicide tonight."

"Here?"

"In this house. On the third floor."

He was a little man, known among the nurses and hospitals for his polite bedside manner and his outside-the-door irritability, a combination not so rare in the profession as unpleasant. And I think he had hoped to impress me with his news. I merely nodded, however, and that annoyed him.

"I'll go on up," I said quietly.

The Inspector was in the hall, but he only glanced

15

at me and looked away, after his usual custom when I take a case for him. The Medical Examiner for the department similarly ignored me. It was an officer in uniform who took my bag and led me up the stairs.

"Bad business, miss," he said. "The old lady went up to see if he had come in, and she found him."

I found myself thinking hard as I followed him. If it was suicide, then what was Inspector Patton of the Homicide Squad doing there? And why had I been called? Any nurse would have answered. Why get me?

"How did he do it?" I asked.

"Shot himself in the forehead," he replied, with a certain unction. "Knelt in front of the mirror to do it. Very sad case."

"Very sad, indeed," I said, thinking of that girl in the drive, and the look of terror in her face. She must have suspected something of the sort, I thought. And later she would call up, and I would have to tell her.

I felt somewhat shaken as I went into the room adjoining the large front bedroom to take off my coat. As I did so, I could hear voices from the other room. One was the low monotonous voice of the very deaf, the other shrill and hysterical.

"Now don't you talk, Miss Juliet. He's all right now. Past all his troubles, and safe in his Maker's arms."

Then something again that I could not hear, and the shrill voice again.

"I've told you over and over. It was an accident. He hadn't the nerve, and you know it. He'd been cleaning his gun. I saw him at it when I went in to turn down his bed, at eight o'clock."

It was evident that they did not know of my arrival, and when I was ready, I did not go at once into the

16

bedroom. Instead, I slipped out quietly and made my way to the third floor. That, too, was lighted, and through an open doorway I saw a policeman sitting on a chair reading a newspaper, and a body lying on the floor. It looked callous to me, but of course there was nothing for him to do, until that conclave ended downstairs in the hall. The room was still filled with acrid smoke, as though flashlight pictures had only recently been taken, and the one window in the room was open, apparently to clear the air.

It was a small room, plainly furnished, a back room, looking toward the service wing at the rear. Later on I was to know that room well: the small white iron bedstead, the old-fashioned bureau, the closet beside the fireplace. But at that moment my eyes were riveted on the body lying on the floor.

It was Herbert Wynne, beyond a doubt. He lay in a curiously crumpled position on his side, with his knees bent and one arm outstretched. There was no weapon whatever in sight.

The officer looked up, and rather shamefacedly laid his paper on the bed. "Better not come in, miss," he said. "Inspector's orders. I'm sorry."

"I haven't any idea of coming in. Have you seen the cook? I shall need some hot water."

"I haven't seen her, miss."

But I lingered in the doorway, staring at that body. "I suppose there's no question about its being suicide?"

"Suicide or accident, I'd say miss."

None of the men, outside of the Bureau itself, knew me or my connection with it. So I assumed an air of ignorance.

"It's terrible, isn't it? I didn't know they took

pictures after suicide? Or even after an accident."

"There'll be an inquest," he said, as though that answered the question, and picked up his paper again. That closed the discussion, but my interest was thoroughly aroused. I knew as well as though I had seen them that the Homicide Squad had been there, working with their rubber gloves, their steel tape measures, their magnifying glasses, their finger-printing outfits. Accident or suicide, and the Homicide Squad on the job!

It was still not much after half past one when I started down the stairs again. Just in time, for Doctor Stewart was fussily on his way up from the lower floor. I could see his bald head and, in the brilliant light, that it was beaded with perspiration. Indeed, he stopped on the landing to mop it, and that gave me time to get safely into Miss Juliet's room. She was lying in her wide old walnut bed, raised high on pillows, and a pallid neurotic-looking little woman of fifty or thereabouts was sitting beside her and holding one of her hands. She got up when she saw me, and stepped back.

"She's getting quieter, miss," she said. "You'll have to speak loud. She's deaf."

It took me only a second, however, to realize why Miss Juliet was quieter. She had lapsed into a coma, and she was almost pulseless.

"Doctor!" I called. "Doctor!"

He hurried then, and for the next few minutes we were two pretty busy people. He ordered a hypodermic of nitroglycerin, and stood for some time holding her pulse and watching it. Not until it perceptibly improved did he speak at all.

"That's curious," he said at last. "She's shown

18

shock, of course. Been restless, and the usual flushed face and rapid pulse. There's a bad heart condition, an arteriosclerosis of the coronary arteries. But she was quieter when I went downstairs. You don't know of anything that could have excited her?"

"I've just come in, doctor."

"How about you, Mary?"

"I don't know. I was just talking to her."

"You didn't say anything to excite her?"

She shook her head. Miss Juliet had been growing calmer as she talked to her; then suddenly she had given a little cry and sat up in bed. She had even tried to get out, and asked for her slippers. Then she apparently changed her mind and lay back again.

"Did she say why she wanted her slippers?"

"I think she wanted to go upstairs again. To see *him.*"

"She didn't explain that?"

"No."

Doctor Stewart considered that, his hand still on the old lady's wrist.

"You didn't intimate to her that he had killed himself?"

"Killed himself! Why should I? He was yellow, through and through. He never killed himself. It was an accident."

All this time she was looking at me with unfriendly eyes. I am used to that, the resentment of all servants, and especially of old servants, to a trained nurse in the house. But it seemed to me that she was not so much jealous of me that night as afraid of me, and that she was even more shrill than usual in her insistence of an accident.

"Why shouldn't she get weak and faint?" she

19

demanded. "She's had a plenty. And not only tonight," she added darkly.

It was some time before the old lady rallied, and still later before the doctor felt that he could safely go. He left me some amyl-nitrite ampoules and nitroglycerin for emergency, and I thought he looked worried as I followed him into the hall.

"Curious," he said, "her collapsing like that. She'd had a shock, of course, but she was all over it; and she wasn't fond of the boy. She had no reason to be. I'm still wondering if Mary didn't say something that sent her off. You see, we've maintained to her that it was an accident. If she learned that it was suicide, or might be, that would account for it."

"I heard Mary telling her it was an accident."

"In that case . . ." He left the sentence unfinished, for one of the men who had been in the lower hall had started up the stairs. He moved slowly and weightily, and I recognized him as he approached us; a well-known attorney in town, named Glenn. He stopped on the landing.

"How is she?"

"Not so well. Better than a few minutes ago, but that's about all."

"Do you think I'd better stay?"

"If anybody stays, I'm the logical one," said the doctor. "But the nurse is here."

Mr. Glenn looked at me for the first time. As I said, I knew him by sight; one of those big-bodied men who naturally gravitate to the law and become a repository for the family secrets of the best people. He looked at me and nodded amiably.

"So I see. Well, I might as well go home; I suppose there is nothing I can do up there." He indicated the

20

third floor.

"They won't let you in, Mr. Glenn," I said. But he was not listening.

"See here, Stewart," he said, "have you any idea why he would do such a thing? Has he been speculating?"

"What did he have to speculate with?" the doctor demanded, rather sourly.

"I suppose that's true enough. How about a girl?"

"Don't ask me. That's your sort of business, not mine!"

Mr. Glenn smiled a little, and put his hand on the doctor's shoulder. "Come, come, Dave," he said, "you're letting this get under your skin. It's bad business, but it's not yours."

They went down the stairs together, companionably enough, and soon afterward the Inspector came up to tell me to close the door from Miss Juliet's room into the hall. The door beside her bed opened close to the foot of the third-floor staircase, and they were about to bring the body down. Mary was still in the room, and I had no chance for a word with him.

Soon after that I heard the shuffling of the men in the hall, and Mary gave a gasp and went very pale. With a sort of morbid curiosity, however, she went out into the hall, after they had passed, and a few moments later she burst back into the room.

"Hugo!" she said. "They've taken him along, miss!"

"Who is Hugo?"

"My husband. What do the police want with him? He doesn't know anything. He was asleep in the bed beside me when Miss Juliet banged on that door out there."

I tried to quiet her. Miss Juliet was apparently asleep, and I was ready myself to get some rest. But she went on and on. Why did the police want Hugo? Mr. Herbert had killed himself. There he was, lying on the floor with his own gun beside him, in front of the bureau. Maybe he meant to, maybe he didn't. Hugo knew nothing. He had almost dropped when he saw the body.

I gathered, here and there through this hysterical outburst, that Hugo and Mary were the only servants in the house, and that they had been there for many years. In the old days Hugo had been the butler and Mary the cook. There had been other servants, but one by one they had drifted away. Now Hugo was everything from houseman to butler, and Mary "was worked until at night she was like to drop off her feet."

I finally got her to bed. It developed that she and Hugo occupied two rooms, a sitting room and bedroom, beyond the second-floor landing; rooms originally used by the family, so that a door on the landing connected with them. But as that door was kept locked as well as bolted, I had to take her downstairs and wait in the kitchen until she had had time to climb the rear staircase.

And it was while I was standing there that I thought I heard, somewhere outside, a soft movement in the shrubbery just beyond the kitchen door.

I put it down to nerves or maybe to a dog, but I did not like it. Standing there in the dark, it seemed to me that something was moving along the kitchen wall outside, and brushing against it.

CHAPTER III

Like all women, I feel safer with a light. Again and again, Mr. Patton has warned me against that obsession.

"Think it over," he said dryly one day. "What is the idea anyhow? It's what is left of your little-girl fear of ghosts, and you know it. But in this business you're not dealing with ghosts; you're dealing with people, and often enough people with guns. Keep dark. Don't move. Don't speak."

But no advice in the world would have kept me from feeling about for the light in that kitchen, and turning it on. It was the light which gave me courage, so that I threw open the kitchen door. And sure enough there was something there. A huge black cat stalked in with dignity, and proceeded to curl up under the stove.

I closed and bolted the door again, but I was still uncertain. I could almost have located that sound I had heard, and it was high up on the frame wall, about shoulder height, I thought. Or maybe that is what some people call hindsight. I know now that it was not the cat, and so I think that I noticed it then.

23

However that may be, I put out the light and went upstairs, as the Inspector put it later on, as though I had been fired out of a gun! I imagine that was at half past two or thereabouts. I know that it seemed incredible, when I had taken off my uniform and put on my dressing gown, to find that it was only three o'clock. It seemed to me that I had been in that old house for hours.

Miss Juliet was sleeping quietly by that time, and her pulse and general condition were much better. In spite of my recent fright, I went methodically enough about my preparation for what was left of the night. But I was still puzzled. As I made my bed on the couch at the foot of Miss Juliet's big bed, as I laid out my hypodermic tray in the front room adjoining, which had been assigned to me, I was still wondering. Both Doctor Stewart and Mr. Glenn had taken it for granted that Herbert Wynne had killed himself by accident or design. Then what did they make of the Homicide Squad? Or did they know about it? I had seen the Inspector slip in a half-dozen men from the Bureau, under the very noses of the family, and nobody suspect it at all.

And had that been the cat, outside in the shrubbery?

The house was eerie that night. There was no wind, but it creaked and groaned all about me; and after I had raised the windows, the furniture began to rap. I knew well enough what it was, that the change of temperature was doing it. But it was as though some unseen hand were beating a fine tattoo, on the old walnut bureau, on the old brass fire irons, even on the footboard of the bed at my head.

24

I must have dozed, in spite of all that, for it was only slowly that I became aware of a still louder rapping, and roused to discover that someone was throwing gravel from the drive against a window sash.

I recognized the signal, and went downstairs at once, to find the Inspector on the front porch. There was still no sign of dawn, but I could see him faintly by the distant light of a street lamp.

"How is she? Asleep?"

"Sound. The doctor gave her a sedative."

He sat down on a step, pulled out his pipe and lighted it.

"Well, here's the layout," he said, "and I'm damned if I know what to make of it. So far as I can learn, young Wynne ate his dinner in good spirits, and spent the time until almost nine o'clock cleaning and oiling his automatic. The cook went in at eight o'clock to turn down his bed, and he was at it, and cheerful enough, she says. Shortly before nine o'clock, Hugo, the butler, heard him go out. He and Mary are man and wife; they occupy the rooms behind the landing on the second floor, and the sitting room is just behind the landing. There's a door connecting it, but it is kept locked and bolted, and the bolt is on the landing side. It's still locked and bolted, for that matter.

"But the point is that Hugo, reading his paper in the sitting room, heard him go down the front stairs shortly before nine o'clock, and says that he was whistling. We can't shake that story of his, and it's probably true. In other words, if we had nothing else to go on, it wouldn't look like suicide."

25

"But you have something else?"

"We have, Miss Pinkerton."

He did not tell me at once, however, and from the way he pulled at his pipe I gathered that something had annoyed him. Finally it came out. Between his department and the District Attorney's office was a long-standing feud, and now it turned out that the District Attorney was already butting in, as he put it; had put on his clothes and appeared himself.

"Afraid he won't get into the papers," he said disgustedly. "Ready to blab the whole story, and steal the job. He's working on Hugo now, so I got out. He leaves all the dirty work to us, but when it comes to a prominent family like this—"

He checked himself, grinning sheepishly and went on. The local precinct station had received a call at fifteen minutes after twelve, and the police lieutenant who first arrived on the scene had merely taken in the general picture, and had decided then and there that it had been suicide.

"Fellow's a fool," the Inspector said. "How do you get a suicide without contact marks? And it's the first hour that counts in these cases. The first five minutes would be better, but we don't get those breaks very often."

"And there were no powder marks on the body?"

"Not a mark. It took O'Brien ten minutes to notice that! And he calls himself a policeman."

He had noticed it finally, however, and he had telephoned to Headquarters.

Luckily the Inspector had still been in his office, and he got to the house at a quarter before one. It took him just two minutes, he said with some pride, to decide that it was neither a suicide nor an accident, to send for the Squad and to telephone for me.

"Not so easy, that last," he said. "Stewart had some pet or other he wanted to put on the case. Yes, Stewart was there. He got there before I did. But I tipped the word to the Medical Examiner, and he told Stewart he had somebody he could get at once. It worked."

"It did," I said grimly. "And what was it that you saw in two minutes?"

"This. That boy was drilled through the center of the forehead; and he didn't move a foot after the bullet hit him. That's certain. But where was he when they found him? He was in front of the bureau, on the floor. All right. O'Brien sized it up first that he'd been standing in front of the mirror, with a revolver pointed at the center of his forehead. But in that case where would the bullet go? It would go through his skull and into the wall at the head of the bed. But it did nothing of the sort. It hit the brick facing of the fireplace, at right angles to the bed, and bounced off. I found it on the floor."

I considered that. It was a ghastly sort of picture at best. "Maybe he didn't face the mirror," I suggested.

"Maybe not. But it's a cinch that he was standing up, if he did it himself. There's no chair in front of that bureau. And that bullet went through his head in a straight line, and hit the fireplace about four feet above the floor. He was pretty close to six feet tall, so you see what I mean."

"He might have knelt."

"Good for you. So he might. They hate the idea of falling, and I've known them to put a blanket on the

27

floor, or a bunch of pillows. I grant you, too, that that would account for the way his knees were bent. But I still want to know why he shows no contact marks. A man doesn't drill himself through the head without leaving something more than just a hole. Of course it's possible that he'd rigged up a device of some sort for firing the gun at a distance, and there's the chance that the servants and the old lady did away with it. They had time enough before they called the police."

"It isn't an insurance case?" I asked. I had worked on one or two such cases for him.

"Well, he had some insurance. The family doctor, Stewart, says he examined him not long ago for a couple of small policies. But why would he do such a thing? Kill himself in order to leave his insurance to an old woman who hadn't long to live, and who didn't like him anyhow? It's not reasonable."

Well, it was not reasonable, and I knew it; although the trouble some people take to kill themselves so that it will look like something else is extraordinary. I believe there is a clause in most policies about suicide; if the holder kills himself within a year, the policy lapses. Something of that sort, anyhow.

"It couldn't have been an accident?" I asked.

"Well, apparently the boy belonged to a pistol club at college; he knew how to handle a gun. And most accidents of that sort occur when the cleaning is going on; not two or three hours later. He'd cleaned that gun before he went out, and left the oil and the rags on top of his bureau. But here's another thing. How do you get an accident with all the earmarks of suicide? Gun on the floor, bent knees as though he might have knelt in front of the mirror, and a bullet straight through his forehead? Straight, I'm telling you. Where was that gun and where was he, in that case?"

"If you're asking me," I said mildly, "I haven't any idea."

He shook out his pipe. "That's what I like about you," he said, smiling into the darkness. "I can talk, and you haven't any theories. You've got a factual mind, and no nonsense."

"What does the Medical Examiner think?"

"He's guessing accident. Stewart is guessing suicide."

"And you?"

"Just at the minute I'm guessing murder. I may change that, of course. But this boy was weak, and it takes more than a temporary spell of depression for any man to plan a suicide so that it looks like something else. Take that gun now; it's the one that killed him. It had been fired since he cleaned it, and there are no prints on it, except some smudged ones that look like his own. Either he'd rigged it so that he could pull a string and fire it from a distance; or somebody else held it with a handkerchief, or wore gloves."

"Nobody heard the shot?"

"Nobody. But that doesn't mean anything. The servants were pretty far away. And the old lady is deaf as a post. There was a shot fired, that's certain. Stewart, who got there before our man, says Wynne hadn't been dead for too long then; less than an hour. The Medical Examiner put the time as about a quarter past eleven. But they're both guessing. So am

I. But I'm guessing that, if it's murder, it's an inside job."

He struck a match and looked at his watch. "Well, the D. A. will be wanting a little shut-eye about now. I'll go back and take over Hugo."

"What do you mean by an inside job?" I demanded. "That old woman, and two antiquated servants! Was there anyone else in the house?"

"Not a soul, apparently. And get this. Even if I can figure that this boy could kill himself without leaving any contact marks, I've got to explain one or two things to myself. Why did he go out whistling at nine o'clock, if he did, and then come back to kill himself at something after eleven? And why did he have a new suitcase in his closet, locked in and partially packed? He was going on a journey, but it wasn't one where he needed silk pajamas!"

Somehow that made me shudder, and he was quick to see it.

"Better go in and get to bed, young lady," he said kindly. "I'm going to need you on this case; I don't want you getting sick. I'll tell you the old lady's story in the morning."

But I refused to go until I had heard it. I did agree to go up and look at my patient, however, and to get my cape to throw about me. I found Miss Juliet quiet and her pulse much better, but, although she kept her eyes closed, I had an idea that she was not asleep.

When I went down again, the Inspector was sitting on the porch step in a curiously intent position, apparently listening to something I could not hear. He waved a hand at me for silence, and then, suddenly and without warning, he bolted around the side of the house. It was a full five minutes before he returned, and he appeared rather chagrined.

"Guess I need some sleep," he said. "I'd have sworn I heard somebody moving back there among the bushes."

It was then that I told him of my own experience earlier in the night, and he made another round of the place without discovering anything. But he did not sit down again; he stood and listened for some little time, his body and ears still evidently on the alert. There was no further sound, however.

I often think of that scene. The two of us there on the front porch, the Inspector's two excursions to the rear, and neither one of us suspecting that a part of the answer to our mystery was perhaps not more than fifty feet away from us while we talked. Or that he almost fell over it in the darkness, without even knowing that it was there.

CHAPTER IV

It was after those interruptions that he relaxed somewhat, and began to do what I often think proves my only real value to him; to use me as an opportunity to think out loud.

"I want to go back to that room again, Miss Adams. No, don't move. I'm not going upstairs. Let's just think about it. Here's this boy, Herbert. Let's suppose something like this. He is sitting in a chair; sitting, because the bullet struck the fireplace at about that height. And he has started to undress, for we found that one shoe was unfastened. The door was closed, we'll say. He sees it opening, but as it was Miss Juliet's custom to discover whether or not he had come in, he does not get up. In a minute, however, he sees that it is not Miss Juliet, but someone else. Still he does not get up. Mind you, if I'm right, he was shot as he sat in that chair, and that chair was in the center of the room, between the hall door and the fireplace. Now, what do you make of that?"

"That he knew whoever it was, or that he had no time to get up."

I felt that he was smiling once more, there in the darkness. "Who says you are not a detective?" he asked. "Someone he knew, probably, if this theory holds at all. He may have been surprised; very likely he was. But he wasn't scared. He was young and active, and he'd have moved in a hurry if he had seen any reason to. He didn't; and get this. Unless we learn to the contrary tomorrow, whoever shot him didn't kill him right off. He had to get into the room and get that gun, for one thing. It was probably on the bureau, and this person picked it up. Then he walked toward the door, turned to go, wheeled and fired. Herbert never knew what hit him."

It was a horrible picture, any way one looked at it, and I felt a little sick. I've seen death in a good many forms, and some of them none too pleasant; but the thought of that boy in his chair, totally unaware that he was breathing his last breath, was almost too much for me. Breathing his last breath and looking up at someone he knew.

"Then it's your idea that, if there was a murder, whoever did it, did it on impulse?" I asked. "If he used Herbert's gun, that looks as though he had none of his own."

"We'll know tomorrow, but I am betting that he used Herbert's gun. As for doing it on impulse, well—maybe, and maybe not. Why was this unknown sneaking into the house at that hour? If we knew that, we could get somewhere. And how did he get in? There are three doors on the lower floor, and all of them were found bolted on the inside, as well as locked. That is, two of them were bolted. The third one, a side entrance, leads into the kitchen, and that is

34

locked off at night. It also leads to the back stairs, but they go up into the servants' sitting room. Nowhere else."

"By a window?"

"Well, Hugo claims to have found a window open all right. But I doubt it. It looks to me as though Hugo, knowing that the house was always locked up like a jail at night, and wanting a murderer, had opened that window. He was a little too quick in discovering it and showing it off. But it happens that the ground is soft outside, and there are no footprints under that window. So I'll stake my reputation, such as it is, that no one got in or out of that window tonight; and that Hugo himself opened it, after the body was discovered."

"But why?" I said bewildered.

"Listen, little sister. If this boy had insurance, the last thing Hugo wants is a verdict of suicide. If Hugo killed him, he's got to show it's an outside job. There are two reasons for you! I could think of others if you want them."

"Then Hugo did it?"

"Not too fast! Let's take the other side for a minute. To do that, we have to figure how somebody unknown could have got into this house tonight and left it, through three doors, all locked, two of them bolted on the inside. And why whoever killed Herbert Wynne killed him with his own gun as he sat in a chair between the fireplace and the door, and moved the body later so that it would look like a suicide."

"And it wasn't Hugo?"

"Think again. Why should he move that body?"

"I've told you I'm no detective," I said briefly. "You'd better tell me. It will save time. I suppose Hugo or somebody in the house could have moved it."

"Why? To make it look like a suicide, when everybody in this house stood to lose if the coroner's verdict at the inquest was suicide? Nonsense!"

"Then whoever killed him moved it?"

"Possibly. We only have two guesses, and that's the other one. Right now I think that is what happened; I believe that Hugo made one attempt to indicate a murder, but that he didn't touch the body. Miss Juliet apparently ordered them to stay out and leave everything as it stood. God knows what he'd have done otherwise, in his anxiety to prove it wasn't suicide. He did manage, however, to get that window in the library open."

"You've been over the ground around the house, of course?"

"Combed it with a fine-toothed comb," he said, and yawned. "Found the point of a woman's high heel just off the drive near the entrance, but too far from the house. Of course, we have to allow for that, too. He wasn't good medicine for women."

Strange as it seems now, for the first time during that talk of ours I remembered the girl in the drive, and told him about her. He was less impressed, however, than I had anticipated, although he stood in thoughtful silence for some time before he made any comment.

"We'll have to watch out," he said, "or we'll be hearing more people in the bushes! I'll admit that this girl looks important, but is she? It isn't unusual these days for a girl to be out alone at one o'clock in the morning, especially if she has a car. Although the car is only a guess, isn't it?"

"I'm convinced it was hers."

"All right. Far be it from me to dispute any hunch of yours. Now what about her? She knows Herbert; maybe she has been playing around with him; tonight she is driving along this street, and she sees a house not notorious for light blazing from roof to cellar. She leaves her car, walks into the drive and discovers a police car near the front door and a crowd of policemen inside the open door. She wouldn't need to be a detective to know that something had happened, would she?"

"It was more than that. She suspected what had happened. It was written all over her."

"And she wouldn't give her name?"

"No. She said she would telephone. But she hasn't."

"But that doesn't look as though she knew when she talked to you, does it? As for not telephoning, perhaps she didn't need to. We've had reporters here, or she may have stopped the doctor on his way out. Depend on it, she knows now or she'd be hanging on the wire."

"Why wouldn't she come to the house and ask?"

"I don't know, but I'll find out tomorrow—today, rather. She ought not to be hard to locate. She may simply have wanted to keep out of the picture, but we can't afford to leave her out. And while this Wynne youth was a pretty bad actor, he was also pretty well known. We'll pick her up, all right, and take her for a little ride."

Before he left, he told me Miss Juliet's story, and tragic enough it seemed to me. She had gone asleep at ten or thereabouts, and slept soundly until ten minutes to twelve. She wakened then, and looked at the clock beside her bed. She was certain of the time, and she sat up, prepared to go upstairs and ascertain if Herbert had come in. This was her nightly custom; to see if he was in the house, and then to go down and examine the front door, to be sure that he had closed it properly.

"Sometimes he came in a little under the weather," the Inspector explained here. He had certain curious reserves of speech with me. "From drinking, you know."

By which I gathered that now and then Herbert had returned to his home in no fit condition even for my experienced ears!

But while Miss Juliet sat there in her bed, looking at her clock, she was aware that someone was walking past her door, in the hall outside. She heard nothing, naturally, but like all very deaf people she was sensitive to vibrations, and her walnut bed was shaking as it always did under such conditions.

She called out. "Herbert! Is that you, Herbert?"

There was no answer, and, with the terror of burglars always in her mind, she was too frightened at first to get out of her bed. She managed that at last, and, feeling no more vibrations, she even opened her door an inch or two. There was nobody in sight, but on the landing above, Herbert's door was open and his light going.

She called again, more sharply, and finally put on her slippers and dressing gown and climbed to the

38

third floor. All she had expected to find was that the boy had gone to sleep with his light burning, and apparently she went up with a sense of outrage at his indifference to waste.

What she saw, from the staircase, had sent her shrieking down to hammer on the door into the servants' rooms at the back. That door was locked, had been locked for years, and was bolted, too. To reach her, the servants had had to go down their own back staircase, through the lower hall and up to where she still stood, hysterically banging at that door.

She led the way back toward the upper room, but she did not go in. Hugo had done so, while she and Mary remained outside. She had told him not to touch anything, and she was certain that he had not done so. The body was lying as the police had found it, in front of the bureau, with the automatic beside it. Yes, the window was open, but it was three full stories above the ground.

She had fainted, or had a heart attack, at about that time, but she remembered that Hugo had said there were no powder marks, and that it must have been an accident. She had asked him then to telephone for Arthur Glenn, her attorney, and Mary had apparently sent for Doctor Stewart, for he arrived shortly after the police from the station house.

That was practically all, but the Inspector added that she had seemed anxious to believe that it was an accident and not suicide.

It was after four o'clock in the morning when he left, getting into his car and driving off at his usual furious speed. I had followed him out into the drive.

"And what am I to do?" I asked.

"Just as usual. Keep your eyes open, that's all. By the way, I've told them to stay out of that room. I want to look it over in the morning."

He put his foot on the starter, but I had thought of something.

"This boy, Herbert, he had a key, of course?"

"To the front door. Yes."

"Could he have brought someone in with him?"

"Not if Hugo is telling the truth, and why shouldn't he? He would give his neck to prove that Herbert Wynne had done just that. But what does Hugo say? He says that he was still in his sitting room beyond the landing at eleven or a little after, that he heard the boy going up the stairs to the third floor, and that he is certain he was alone."

Then he roared away, and I was left standing in the drive alone.

It was still dark, although there was a hint of dawn in the sky. Dark and cold. I shivered a little as I turned back and went into the house again.

Upstairs, old Miss Juliet still lay very quietly in that great walnut bed, her head high so she could breathe more easily, but I still had that odd feeling that she was only pretending to be asleep.

I stood and looked down at her. How old she was I have no idea even now; in her late seventies, I imagine. Possibly eighty. There were stories that Miss Juliet Mitchell had been a great beauty in her day, but there were no signs of that beauty now. She looked infinitely old and very weary. It seemed to me, as I looked at her, that surely age should have certain compensations for what it has lost, and that peace and comfort should be among them. But I wondered if she had not grown hard with the years. I was remembering what the Inspector had quoted as her words when she had finished her statement.

"He is dead," she had said, "and I will speak no evil of him. But if someone murdered him, it was for good cause. I knew him well enough to know that. And he never killed himself. He had not the courage."

CHAPTER V

It was well after four in the morning when I finally lay down and tried to get an hour's sleep on a couch at the foot of the old lady's bed. It was hard to do. She was apparently asleep, but it grew still cooler toward dawn, and if before, everything about that ancient house had seemed to creak, now it appeared to me as I lay there that ghostly figures were moving up and down the stairs. Once a curtain blew out into the room and touched me on the hand, and I had all I could do not to yell my head off.

I must have dozed again, but only for a short time. I was roused by an odd sort of vibration of the footboard of the big bed; my sofa was pushed against it, so it was shaking also.

What with the Inspector's story of some loose floor boarding or joist which connected with the hall outside, I knew what that meant, and I sat up with a jerk. Over the high footboard I could see Miss Juliet's bed, and it was empty!

I was still sitting there, gasping, when I heard the door to the hall open cautiously, and saw her come feebly back into the room. She was ghastly white, and she stopped and stood motionless when she saw me. She was in her nightgown and her feet were bare. I dare say the fright had made me irritable, for I jumped up and confronted her.

"You know you shouldn't have got out of bed, Miss Mitchell," I said sternly. "That's what I'm here for."

Whether she heard me or not, she understood my attitude.

"I've been walking off a cramp in my leg," she said in her flat, monotonous voice. "Do lie down, and go to sleep again. I'm quite all right."

She moved toward the bed, and, dark as the room still was, I felt certain that she held something in the hand I could not see, and that, with a surprisingly quick gesture, she slid it under a pillow. Right or wrong—and I know now that I was right—she refused any help in getting back into bed, or to allow me to straighten her bedclothing, or, indeed, to work about the bed at all.

"Let me alone, please," she said when I attempted it. "I don't like being fussed over."

She could not, however, prevent my putting a heater to her feet, and seeing that the soles were soiled; or taking her pulse and discovering that it was extremely fast, or watching her breathing, which was rapid and labored. Nor could she impose on me by pretending to be asleep until Mary came to relieve me for my breakfast. Neither one of us slept a wink from that time on, and I suppose there was a certain humor, hard to discover at the time, in my occasional cautious peerings over the foot of that bed, my hair flying in all directions and my very face swollen with

44

lack of sleep; and Miss Juliet's equally wary watching, and the closing of her eyes the moment she saw the top of my head rising beyond that walnut footboard.

Whatever she had under her pillow, I did not get it, for Mary relieved me at eight for breakfast, a slim meal served by a morose Hugo in a shabby coat, with purple pouches of sheer exhaustion under his eyes. If there had been suppressed indignation for that night of interrogation in Mary's manner as she relieved me, there was a curious look of humiliation in his. He looked old, tired and rather pathetically shamed.

"I'm afraid you had a hard night, Hugo."

"I suppose it was to be expected, miss."

He did not care to talk, I saw, and so I let him alone. But as I ate my toast and drank my weak tea, I had a chance to see more fully the impoverished gentility of that house. No wonder, if the Wynne boy had actually killed himself, Hugo had tried to make it look like a murder. The threadbare carpets, the thin and carefully darned table linen, the scanty food served with such ceremony, all pointed to a desperate struggle to keep up appearances.

And to save my life I could not see Herbert Wynne in that house. He had come and gone, apparently leaving no more impression on it than if he had never been.

Mary was still in Miss Juliet's room when I went up again. The door was closed, so I had a moment or two in which to get my bearings by daylight. I could see that the house was only three stories in the front, and that the back wing, including the kitchen, the pantry and, as I discovered later, the laundry, was only two.

This back wing, a later addition, was of frame, while the main body of the house was brick. It was above the kitchen and so on that the servants had their rooms, carefully locked off and bolted from the landing on the front stairs. And it was evident that only the main staircase led to the third floor. The rear one, as Inspector Patton has said, led only to the two rooms and bath used by Mary and Hugo.

The house itself was a double house; that is, there was a long center hall leading back to the pantry and service quarters. On one side of the hall was a library with a dining room behind it. On the other was what was known as the long parlor. The doors into it were closed, but I knew that it was there. It had been rather a famous room locally in the old days, with its two crystal chandeliers and its two fireplaces, each with a marble mantel and a mirror over it.

On the second floor, not counting the locked-off rooms where Mary and Hugo lived, were three bedrooms. One of them, a small room behind Miss Juliet's, was largely dismantled, however, and Miss Juliet's was what used to be called the main chamber. It lay over the library and the lower hall along the front of the house, and opened onto the upper hall. My own room was next to it, also along the front of the house, but smaller, with a window at the rear as well as at the front and side.

The third floor, as I discovered later, was not greatly unlike the second, save that the ceilings were lower.

That morning, however, I had only time to glance at the lower floor, and on my way upstairs to stop and examine the door leading back into the servants' wing. I remembered something the Inspector had told me: that the outside door at the foot of the back stairs, the stairs which led to this wing, was the only one which lacked a bolt. In that case, the only exit which could have been made, outside of the windows, would have been by that door with its spring lock. But as that side entrance led only into a small entry, with a door to the kitchen which the servants locked each night, carrying the key upstairs with them by Miss Juliet's orders, and to the staircase by which they reached their rooms, it appeared to me that this door on the landing might have some strategic value.

But that door offered nothing. It was both locked and bolted, and the bolt was shoved home in plain sight, as the Inspector had said. Clearly no one could have left the house by that door, and bolted it behind him.

As a matter of fact, my inspection of that door very nearly got me into trouble that morning. I had just time to stoop and pretend to be tying my shoe when Mary opened Miss Juliet's door. But I thought she looked at least as frightened as I felt when she saw me, and as she scurried past me, I was convinced of something else. She was holding something under her apron.

I watched her down the stairs, and at the foot she stopped and looked back at me. Like Miss Juliet and myself the night before, we must have presented a curious little tableau for that second; but in my position suspicion is fatal, and so I turned and started back to Miss Juliet. It was then that the doorbell rang, and, listening carefully, it seemed to me that Mary just inside the front parlor, did not answer it at once; that there was a quick movement of some sort, perhaps by the library door. But I could not be certain, and almost immediately I heard the front door opened.

It was Mr. Glenn, stopping on his way to his office to inquire about the old lady. I went down myself to tell him of her condition, and thus interrupted Mary in a flood of indignation over Hugo's experience at Headquarters. He looked annoyed himself.

"Of course it's an outrage," he said. "I'll see that it isn't repeated, Mary. And I'll talk to Hugo. You'd better get him."

Having thus got rid of her for the moment, he turned to me. But he was still irritable. "Trust the police to make a mess of it," he said. "Hugo's been with Miss Mitchell for thirty years. That ought to prove something. And what are the police after, anyhow? Either Herbert Wynne killed himself or he met with an accident. There's nothing for the police in either case. How is Miss Mitchell this morning? Did she sleep?"

"She rested. I don't think she slept much."

He stood there looking about the shabby hall, so old and worn in the morning sunlight, and apparently he felt its contrast with his own prosperous appearance, his neatly shaved face, his good, well-cut clothes, the car in the drive outside. He frowned a little.

"She has had a hard life," he said. "Not that this unfortunate event deprives her of much that she valued, but still . . . Has she talked at all?"

"Not to me."

"We'd like her to think of it as an accident. I suppose you know that?"

"The doctor said so. Yes."

He lowered his voice. "They hadn't been the best of friends, Herbert and Miss Mitchell. If she thought now that he had done away with himself, I doubt if she would survive it. All we can hope is that the coroner will see the light on this case."

Hugo arrived then, and I went back to my patient. I thought she seemed flushed, but she had no fever. When I bathed her—under protest at that, for she wanted Mary to do it—I noticed that the soles of her delicate old feet were now soft and unsoiled, and that puzzled me. Certainly she had been out of the room that early morning and soiled her feet on those carpets, which were not clean. They looked as if the dust of ages were in them.

That mystery was solved, however, when I found a damp washcloth in the bathroom. Either alone or with Mary's help the old lady had removed the traces of that nocturnal journey of hers! Then it had been a journey. There had been no cramp in the leg. She had lied, and I rather thought she was not given to lying.

I said nothing, of course. I changed her bed and her gown, and then stood back.

"Are you comfortable now?"

"Quite comfortable, my dear."

I dare say all nurses grow fond of their patients, if they are given a chance. I do not know just why, unless it is that they appeal to the maternal in us. Or perhaps it is even more than that. For a brief time, a week or a month, we become a bit of God, since it is His peace which we try to bring. But that morning I began to resent my place in that house, with its spying and watching. I wanted to help that poor old woman. And she would not allow me to help her. She

49

never did.

Hugo and Mr. Glenn were still closeted in the library when I had finished, but Mr. Glenn left soon afterward. I could hear them in the hall below, and I thought Hugo's voice sounded more cheerful.

"Goodbye, Hugo."

"Goodbye, sir. I'll do what you say."

As he went out to his car, I saw from the window a man with a camera snapping him. It annoyed him and I could hear him angrily berating the photographer, but the man had got what he wanted. He merely smiled and turned away. As a matter of fact, the place was full of reporters and cameramen of all sorts, and it was a good thing that Miss Juliet could not hear the doorbell, for it rang all morning.

Hugo tried driving them away, but of course we were helpless, and all the noon editions of the papers showed photographs of the house. "FAMOUS OLD MITCHELL MANSION SCENE OF TRAGEDY." Also, a few morbid-minded people had stood by the gate for a part of the morning, but with the news that the body had been taken away, their interest faded, and by noon the place was practically cleared.

Only two things of any importance happened that morning. After the lawyer's departure, Hugo climbed to that room of Herbert's on the third floor, remained there about two minutes and then came down again. Listening, I did not think that he entered the room at all, but stood in the doorway, surveying it.

And after the doctor's visit that morning I prepared for an indefinite stay.

"She's a sick woman, Miss Adams," he said. "She's been a sick woman for years, and she needs care. She

50

couldn't afford it before, but now I imagine she'll be more comfortable. That is, unless some idiotic coroner's jury decides that that poor weakling killed himself."

"There was considerable insurance, then?"

He looked at me thoughtfully. "I don't know how much, but probably enough so that the insurance companies will try to prove a suicide," he said. "It's absurd on the face of it. Why should he insure himself and then kill himself to save from poverty an old woman who hasn't long to live at the best, and for whom he showed no affection whatever?"

"It's made out to her?"

"The only policies I know about were made out to his estate. It's the same thing. He has no other relatives."

"You don't know how much it amounts to?"

"No. But I telephoned Mr. Glenn, Miss Juliet's attorney, early this morning. He's trying to check up on it now. It's a puzzle to me where he got the money to pay for it. Or why he did it at all."

"I suppose it isn't possible that he was trying to repay Miss Mitchell what his father had lost for her?" I asked.

But he fairly snorted at that. "You didn't know him, did you?" was his reply.

Naturally, the police had been around most of the morning. They had ordered the newspapermen to stick to the drive and were combing the grounds carefully. While I was bathing Miss Juliet, the Inspector had entered the house and made a final examination of Herbert's room, and I gathered that he gave Mary permission to put it in order, for later on I heard her sweeping overhead. But I had no chance to talk to him. Once or twice I saw him from a window; accompanied by a plain clothes man, he was moving slowly about the shrubbery, and at one point, near the side door, he spent some time. A little later I saw him standing off and gazing up at Herbert's window, and watched his eyes travel from it to the roof of the rear wing.

But whatever he found, if anything, I had no way of discovering. As I have said, it is one of his rules that he ignores me as much as possible on his cases, and that I use my off-duty either to see or to telephone him. As I usually take eighteen-hour duty when he uses me, I have six hours in which to do either.

I made one or two attempts to get into the library that morning, but they were entirely futile. No sooner had I got there, or even part of the way down the stairs, than some idiotic reporter would ring the doorbell again, and I would hear Hugo on his way to the door. Indeed, I would probably have abandoned the idea altogether if I had not made a rather curious discovery shortly after luncheon.

Mary had relieved me as before, and when I went upstairs again, I smelled something burning. I said nothing about it, but it did not take me long to notice that there were pieces of freshly charred paper in the fireplace, or that there was a pad of paper and a pencil on the old lady's bedside table, beside her glasses.

That renewed my suspicion, naturally. It looked as though Mary, having something to say that she dared not shout, had resorted to writing. And that what she had had to say had been so important that Miss Juliet had ordered her to burn it.

CHAPTER VI

I had plenty to think about after that discovery and I set about to prepare for an indefinite stay: unpacking my suitcase in my own room.

What did they know, these people in the house, about what had happened to Herbert Wynne the night before? "I'm guessing murder," the Inspector had said. Murder by whom? By Miss Juliet? Absurd. By Mary? I considered that. She was one of those small tight-lipped neurotics who sometimes turn to religion and now and then to crime. By Hugo? He worshiped the old lady, and of course there was the insurance.

Yet as I had watched him, old and stooped and shabby, I somehow felt that he was not a killer. Certainly he had that combination which the Inspector regards as the basis of practically all crime, motive and opportunity. But what of that? I have had them myself!

Miss Juliet's condition was only fair that afternoon. She was restless and uneasy, and I felt that she was still watching me. She even showed a certain relief when I said that, while I would not take my

53

regular hours off, I would like to go home and get some street clothes; I had arrived in a uniform. Said, however, is merely a euphemism for the shouts with which I attempted to communicate with her.

"That's all right," she said, when I had finally made her understand. "Don't hurry."

I did not go to Headquarters that day. I telephoned from my apartment instead, and found the Inspector in his office. I thought his voice sounded unusually grave, and he listened intently while I told him of Miss Juliet's excursion, and the discovery of the written messages between the old lady and Mary.

"You think she went up to the third floor?"

"I know she had been somewhere in the house. She hadn't worn her slippers, and when I put a heater to her feet, the soles looked as though she had been about quite a little."

"Then it's your idea that she got something, perhaps from the third-floor room, and passed it on to Mary to hide?"

"It looks like that, Inspector."

"You don't think she went outside the house?"

Well, I hadn't thought of that, although of course it was possible. He explained what he meant. The ground all around the house was hard except under the library windows. There it had been recently spaded under, and as I knew, there were no footprints there. But outside the laundry they had found that morning in a patch of dusty ground what looked like the print of a woman's foot. A small foot, without a shoe.

"Looked as though somebody had been there in her stocking feet," he said. "May not mean anything, of course. What does Mary wear?"

"A flat felt slipper. And her feet are small."

"Well, that's probably what it is. Could you get into the library?"

"No. And what would be the use? Whatever it was, it's probably gone now."

"You have no idea of what it might have been?"

"Something flat, and not heavy, I thought."

"Like a letter?"

"I thought of that. But you had searched the place. If he left a letter, he'd have left it where it could be seen."

He was silent for a perceptible time. "It's the devil of a case," he said at last. "You'd better give the library the once over if you get a chance. And by the way, Glenn—that's the family lawyer; you saw him last night—Glenn has been working on the insurance. There's a lot of it."

"How much?"

"He's not certain," he said, "but he thinks it may amount to a hundred thousand dollars."

I was fairly stunned. Here was a boy who had had no money of his own, and who had earned only a little now and then; he had tried to sell bonds, I knew, and automobiles. But the chances were that he had earned little or nothing since the depression set in, and now here he was shown taking out a hundred thousand dollars of insurance for the benefit of a woman he had disliked, and who had not cared for him.

"But how in the world . . ."

"I don't know. Ask me something easy. Apparently he would deposit sufficient cash in a bank to cover the premium, and then check it out. Most of the policies were small."

He had not a great deal more to say, and I gathered that he was disturbed and not too easy in his mind. The firearms expert of the Bureau had said that the bullet came from Herbert's own revolver, and the fingerprint men that the prints were his, although not clearly readable. There had been no other prints found, in or about the room.

Before I rang off, I asked about the girl of the night before, and while he was confident that they would find her, he had to admit that they were still at sea.

"We'll get her, all right," he said. "But I'm not sure that she's important. By the way, have you got your gun among your things there?"

"No."

"That's right. No telling who may go through your stuff, and I don't want you fired from the case. I have a hunch I'm going to need you." That was his way, to throw out remarks of that sort and not to explain them. I had to put up with it, but I must say my little apartment looked homelike and cheerful to me after that conversation. Dick was singing, and there was my sewing basket, as I had left it, and the thousand and one little things with which I have built such an atmosphere of home as is possible under the circumstances. I sat down for a few minutes, and I don't mind saying that I called myself an idiot for getting involved in other people's troubles. After all, nursing alone is pretty hard work, and when I had added to it the inside job of assisting an Inspector of Police, I had taken on more than I bargained for.

I could see myself in the mirror, and I realized that I

56

looked tired, and older than my age. But that very mirror sent my mind back to the Mitchell case, and with that I was on my feet again, and gathering up what I needed. The game was in my blood, after all.

Before I left, I looked at Dick. He looked little and woebegone, but he chirped as I moved to the closet.

"Want a piece of sugar, Dick?"

He stared back at me, with his head cocked and his eyes glittering like small jet beads.

Well, that was on Tuesday. Herbert Wynne had been found dead late on Monday night, and the inquest was to be the next day, Wednesday. That evening Doctor Stewart, Mr. Glenn and the Inspector held a three-cornered conference in the library, but I had no chance to speak to the Inspector, and nothing new to tell him. At nine o'clock it was over, and the doctor came upstairs and saw Miss Juliet. He left a bromide for me to give her, and by half after ten o'clock she was settled for the night.

That was the first opportunity I had had to search the library, and I took it.

Hugo had looked dead to the world all evening, and by ten o'clock he and Mary had locked up the house and gone to bed. At least, listening at the door on the landing as I went downstairs at eleven o'clock, I could hear nothing.

I had taken my pocket flash along, so that I turned on no lights, and I went at once to the library. It was a dark and dismal room at any time, and I remember that, as I searched, there were innumerable creaks and raps all around me. I would find myself looking over my shoulder, only to face a wall of blackness that seemed to be full of potential horrors.

57

And, not unexpectedly, the search produced nothing. It was not my first experience of the sort for the police, and I flatter myself that I did it pretty well, considering that I had not the faintest idea what I was looking for. I ran my hand down behind the cushions of chairs, felt under the edge of the rug, and even behind the rows on rows of dusty books. But I found nothing at all, save behind the books near the door a scrap of dirty newspaper, which I left—luckily, as it happened—where I had found it.

Just why, after completing this search, I should have decided to investigate the long parlor across the hall I do not know to this minute. I did not believe that Mary had gone in there, for the high old double doors were always kept closed. But I was less nervous by that time, and I own to a certain curiosity as to the room itself. Perhaps it rather pleased me to enter uninvited into a parlor which had been, in its day, so rigidly guarded and so exclusive!

I opened the doors carefully and let my light travel over the room. No trace of its former grandeur remained, however. If the library had been dingy, this once-famous long parlor of the Mitchell house was depressing. It was done in the worst of the later Victorian manner, with figured wallpaper and a perfect welter of old plush chairs and sofas, and there were a number of windows with heavy curtains and an additional one at the rear, looking out over the service wing and the entrance to it.

It was not until my light had traveled to that window that I started. It had never occurred to me that the room might be tenanted. But tenanted it was, and by Hugo. He was sitting, only partially dressed, in a large easy chair just inside the window, and he was sound asleep.

Mysterious as this was, I had no intention of arousing him, so I slipped back into the hall again and closed the doors. I must have turned my light off at that time, for I recall standing in the hall in the dark and listening, afraid I had awakened him. No sound came from the parlor, however, and I proceeded to grope my way up the stairs. I dare say I moved very quietly in my rubber-soled shoes, for my memory is of silence, utter and complete. Silence and black darkness. I know that I was halfway up the stairs when the hall clock began to strike midnight, and that the wheeze it gave before it commenced sent a cold shiver over me. But it was not until I reached the landing that the real shock came.

There was something there on the landing with me, something blacker than the darkness, which moved and swayed in the corner by the door. And not only moved and swayed. It seemed to be coming toward me.

I could hear a voice screaming, but I did not even realize that it was mine. And I must have backed down the stairs, although I have no recollection of that retreat; for when Hugo came running, he stumbled over me, halfway up the stairs. I still remember his ghastly pallor when, having turned on the light, he bent over me and found that I was uninjured. Then he shook me, not too gently.

"What was it? What happened?"

"There was something on the landing. Somebody.

It came at me."

"There's nobody there, miss."

"There was somebody there. I'm not an idiot. Do you think I want to scare myself to death?"

I saw then that he had a revolver in his hand, an old-fashioned single-action gun.

But the careful search which followed revealed nothing whatever. The door on the landing was locked and bolted. Miss Juliet was gently snoring in her bed, and from beyond, in the servants' sitting room, Mary was hysterically demanding to know what was wrong.

We went over the entire house together that night, Hugo and I. It was certain that, if anyone had been on the landing, he could not have passed me to get down the stairs, and so we directed our main attention to the third floor.

There were two front rooms there, unoccupied and sparsely furnished; a small storeroom; and the rear one where Herbert had been killed. But we found nothing in any of them, nor any indication that anybody had entered them. Hugo persisted long after I was willing to abandon the search and to try to get some sleep. He still had his revolver in his hand, but he offered no explanation for it, or for his appearance from the parlor when I screamed.

It was full daylight before I dropped off into an uneasy sleep. My mind was abnormally active and filled with questions. Why had Hugo kept that vigil of his at the parlor window? What did he know that he would not tell, about the whole mystery? And who had been on that landing? For someone had been

60

there. I was willing to stake my reputation on it.

It was not until the next morning at breakfast that Hugo saw fit to enlighten me as to how he had come from the parlor in answer to my scream, and with a revolver at that.

"You may have wondered at my having a gun last night, miss," he said, as he put down my cup.

"I had plenty of things to wonder about," I said dryly.

"I suppose you couldn't describe what it was you saw?"

"It looked like a ghost. I don't suppose that helps any!"

"Tall or short, miss?"

"I was a little excited," I admitted. "It was rather like a tall man, stooping. It was there, and then it wasn't, if that means anything."

There was no question that he was disturbed, and that he was trying to connect what I had seen with what turned out to have been an experience of his own the night before. Briefly, and corroborated by Mary, his story was that both of them had retired shortly after the doctor left. As I have said, the doctor had remained after the others, to pay Miss Juliet his final visit.

At half past ten or thereabouts Hugo had put out the light and gone to raise a window; but that particular window looked down over the rear end of the long parlor, and as he stood there, he thought he saw somebody in the corner below, close up against the wall.

He put on some clothes, took his revolver and went

down the rear staircase. At the side door at its foot he stopped and listened, but he heard nothing, so he groped his way to the parlor and looked out the window there. The room was dark, and he could see nothing suspicious outside. But he was very tired, having had no sleep the night before, and when everything remained quiet, he sat down and finally dropped off.

That was the story, and what I had seen bore it out. But I wondered if it was all of the story, although it was possibly all that Mary knew. It seemed to me that he was vaguely on the defensive, and now and then he glanced at his wife as though for confirmation. Or perhaps to see the effect on her! Who knows, even now? I had an idea that he was not in the habit of confiding in Mary.

The Inspector called me up as I finished breakfast, and after our usual custom when this is necessary, I pretended that he was a doctor.

"Listen," he said, "I want you to do something for me."

"Yes, doctor."

"Take a bit of air this morning, and look close to the house for marks of a ladder; a pruning ladder. I'll explain later."

"I'm terribly sorry," I said, for Hugo's benefit. He was in the dining room. "But I imagine I'll be here for several days. I'd like to take the case for you, however. Don't forget me later on, will you?"

"Do it soon, and come in this afternoon," was his reply. Then he hung up.

The servants and I had agreed to keep the story of

62

the night before from Miss Juliet. She was not so well that morning, and although I did not think she was grieving for the boy, it was as plain as the rather aquiline nose on her face that she was worrying about something. I put it down as anxiety over the inquest, which was to be held that morning. After all, poor old soul, the verdict would mean a great deal to her, and she could not bring the boy back to life. I saw her looking at the clock now and then. She spoke only once, and that was when I had rubbed her back with alcohol.

"You have good hands, my dear."

And once again I detested my job, sneaking into that house under false pretenses and fooling the poor old creature into being even mildly grateful to me. I had to harden myself deliberately, to remember that very probably she had found and hidden an important piece of evidence, before I felt equal to going on with the work. An important piece of evidence, perhaps, for which the detectives for the insurance companies would have given their eyeteeth!

That was on Wednesday. The inquest was to be held at eleven, and both Hugo and Mary left the house at ten thirty that morning. Miss Juliet was drowsing, and so I had an opportunity to make the search the Inspector had ordered without any interested supervision. I had only the faintest idea of what constituted a pruning ladder, but any ladder leaves twin impressions, and so I made my way slowly around the house, beginning at the front door, continuing around the library, the kitchen wing and back to the long parlor.

But I found no ladder marks, and it was at the side door, just behind that rear window, that I passed a clump of shrubbery and suddenly confronted the girl who had stopped me in the drive the night Herbert Wynne was killed. She was standing in the corner, backed up against the wall, and if ever I have seen a girl look scared to death, she did.

CHAPTER VII

She relaxed, however, the moment she saw me.
"Good heavens! I thought they'd come back!"
"Who had come back?"
"The servants. I waited until I saw them go out, and then I slipped in."

Well, I had had time to have a good look at her, and I saw that if she had not looked so utterly stricken, she would have been really beautiful. Now, however, she looked as though she had not slept for a week; her eyes were swollen, and now and then she gave me an odd little defiant look.

"What are you doing here, anyhow?" I asked her.

"I came to see you," she replied rather breathlessly. "After all, you're a nurse. You'll understand, and I have to talk to someone or I'll go crazy. You see, he never killed himself. I don't care what the verdict is. He never did."

"How do you know?"

"Because I knew him very well. I was—engaged to him. And he knew he was in danger."

"What sort of danger? Who from?" I said.

"I don't know. He said he was being followed.

That's why he was cleaning his gun. He said somebody was trying to get him."

"But he must have said something to explain all that."

"He wouldn't tell me. There was something going on, but he wouldn't tell me what it was."

"You haven't told the police?"

She shook her head. "I don't want to be dragged into it," she said. "But he knew it might happen. And he knew something else. He told me once that if anybody got him, they'd try to get me, too."

"But that's ridiculous," I expostulated. "Why should anyone want to kill you? And why do you think that all this wasn't an accident? They do happen, you know."

She shook her head again. "He was murdered," she said, looking at me, her eyes swollen with long crying. "He was murdered, and I know who did it."

I was not so certain that she knew, however, when she had finished her story. But before I let her begin, I made an excuse of going back to Miss Juliet, and did a thing which I loathed, but which was essential. I telephoned to Headquarters and left word that the girl was at the Mitchell place, and to have somebody ready to follow her when she left.

Miss Juliet was quiet when I ran up to her. I suppose she knew that the inquest was being held that morning, but she had not mentioned it to me.

"I'm all right," she said in her flat voice. "You needn't stay in the room. Go out and get some air."

When I went back to the girl, I found her crouched on the doorstep, a small heap of young wretchedness that went to my heart and made me feel guiltier than ever. But she told her story clearly and well.

She had been in love with the dead boy, and he with her. She knew his faults. He was lazy, and not too scrupulous, I gathered, but that had not made any difference, apparently; except that it had caused her people to dislike him, and finally to forbid him at the house. After that, they had had to meet outside, wherever they could. Sometimes they took walks, or drove in her car. She had a small coupé. Sometimes they merely sat and held hands in the movies. I gathered, too, that there was another young man who cared for her, and who was likely to make trouble if he saw her with Herbert, so they had had to choose remote places.

"What sort of trouble?" I asked sharply.

She started and colored, but her chin went up. "Not what you think. That's ridiculous." She looked rather uneasy, however, and she expatiated on this other youth's good qualities at some length. Then she went back to Herbert again.

It appeared that they had been quite happy, until a month or so ago. At that time Herbert had changed. Sometime in the spring he had got a little money, she didn't know where, and had put it into the market on a margin. Stocks were very low, and he had thought he would make some money. But all summer they had remained low, and even dropped. That had worried him.

"But not enough to make him kill himself," she hastened to explain. "He was anxious, but he was sure they would do better this fall. And he didn't worry about money anyhow. He was like that. It was something else. He began to act as though he was

67

afraid of something."

"He didn't say what it was?"

"No. But he said that he was being followed, and that he was in danger of some sort."

"Did he know who it was?"

She hesitated. "He thought it was my father, at first. It was someone who had a car, and of course he knew my family was watching me, or trying to. I knew it wasn't Father; I thought at first that Herbert was just excited. He liked to imagine things, you know. But one night I saw the car myself. It trailed us along a country road. At first I thought it was someone else, but I know now that it wasn't."

"You thought it was the other man, I suppose?"

She nodded. "But it wasn't. It wasn't his car." She looked at me searchingly. "I'm telling you the truth. I knew his car well, and it wasn't his."

"It wasn't your father's?"

"Father and Mother dined out that night, and played bridge. They came in after I did, together."

"Then who was it? Who is it you suspect?"

She looked around before she answered. "Hugo," she said. "Miss Juliet's butler."

"Hugo hasn't got a car. There's no car here."

"He could rent one, couldn't he? Or she could rent one for him."

"But why? Aren't *you* imagining things now?"

"I'm not imagining that Herbert is dead, am I? Look at it! The papers say he had taken out a lot of insurance. Where did he get the money to do that? And why would he do it? He knew they had no use for him. And—maybe you don't know this—that old woman in there was pretty desperate. She was going

68

to be put out of the house."

"But even that . . ."

"You don't know her," she went on, her voice rising. "She hated Herbert. She had hated his father for marrying his mother and then losing her money. And she's proud. She's always been a great lady in this town, and she'd rather kill than have a Mitchell go to the poorhouse. You've seen her. Is she grieving? Is she even decently sorry? You know she's not."

"If she was as desperate as that, how would Miss Juliet have obtained any money to insure Mr. Wynne?"

"I don't know. Maybe Hugo had some. Herbert used to say that he was as tight as the paper on the wall. He'd probably saved a lot."

However all that may be, Herbert had been less depressed for the past ten days. He told her that he was getting everything ready, and that soon they would go away together. He had a plan of some sort, but he didn't say what it was. All he told her was that she was to be ready to go at any time.

"To be married, I suppose?"

"Certainly. What do you think I am?"

I thought she was less frank about this, however. There was a change in her manner. She seemed to be choosing her words. But there seemed to be no doubt as to the essential facts. They were to go away as soon as he could sell his stocks without a loss. He had put five thousand dollars in them.

"Five thousand dollars," I said. "Where did he get it? From Miss Juliet?"

"She's never seen five thousand dollars at one time in her life," she replied scornfully. "No. I don't know

69

where he got it last spring. He just said he had had a windfall. He wasn't very communicative, at any time. I—well, I asked him if he was bootlegging, and he just laughed. He said it was all right, and that the only dealing he'd ever had with a bootlegger was to buy a quart of gin."

Then, about a week before, they had both had a bad fright. They had been motoring along a country road again, and they were both certain that they had not been followed. They had stopped by the side of the road, and he had turned on the light on the instrument board to look at a railroad schedule. They were planning the elopement. Both of them, I gathered, were bent forward so that they saw nothing, but a car raced by them and fired several shots. Neither one was hit, but the glass in the windshield of her coupé had been shattered.

They gave up driving about after that. Herbert was in a bad way. His hands shook and he said he couldn't sleep. For two or three days they did not meet at all, although he called her now and then over the telephone.

"And still you had no explanation of all this?" I asked incredulously.

She hesitated. "I thought it was someone else. But I know now that I was wrong."

"You thought it was the other young man?"

"Well, I did and I didn't. I'd been engaged to him when I met Herbert, and he was pretty bitter about it. After that shooting, of course, I knew it wasn't. He's not that sort at all. And anyhow," she added naïvely, "he wouldn't have risked killing me."

Then came that last night. She told it clearly

enough, although she constantly dabbed at her eyes with a moist ball of handkerchief.

They had met about nine o'clock at a small neighborhood moving-picture theater. Herbert was uneasy, she said, and he told her that he had brought his revolver along. But he would tell her no more than that, and they sat quietly enough through the picture. When they went out, she found that her bag was missing, and she went back and found it, on the floor under her seat. When she emerged again, he had bought a copy of the evening edition of the *Eagle*, and was looking at the financial page.

"It looks as though everything has gone to hell," he said to her, and folded the paper and put it in his pocket. But he did not seem particularly depressed. He put his arm through hers and took her to the corner, and once he turned around and looked back. He seemed satisfied that he was not followed, however, and he put her into her car there, and, leaning in, kissed her good night.

"Just a day or two now," he said, "and we'll be on our way. On our way and sitting pretty!"

He was whistling as he went down the street. And that was the last she ever saw of him.

Up to that final farewell of Herbert's I felt sure that she had been telling the truth, although possibly not all of it. It was when it came to the later incident in the drive, when she had accosted me, that I was less certain.

She had not gone home at all, she said. She often drove about at night by herself, and this night she had had a good bit to think about. Her people did not like Herbert, and she was as good as committed to

71

going away with him in a day or so. She drove out into the country, and somewhere on a remote road she found she had a flat tire. It took a good while to change it, and she was on her way home when she passed the Mitchell house and saw the lights there.

Well, it might have been true. Girls do queer things these days, although a car has to travel a good many miles, even with a flat tire to change, to use up two hours or more. True or not, however, there was no doubt that she believed with every ounce of her that Hugo had killed Herbert Wynne, and that with the tacit agreement of the old woman in the bed upstairs.

But she stubbornly refused to give her name, or to go to the police, although I warned her that they would find her, sooner or later. She only shrugged her shoulders at that.

"Why?" she said. "The verdict will be accidental death, and that closes it, doesn't it?"

"Not necessarily."

"Well, I've told you what I came to tell you. You can pass it on to the police if you like. But tell them to leave me out of it. I'm telling you; they did it." She indicated the house. "And they'd kill me, just as if stepping on a bug, if I got in their way."

All this time, of course, I had been watching for some indication that my message to Headquarters had reached Inspector Patton. Now, as she rose to go, I saw that it had. Across the street and down a half block or so was a dark inconspicuous car, with the engine running. But I felt cheap and unhappy when she turned to me and held out her hand.

"It's done me good just to talk to you," she said.

72

"You see, I have nobody else."

I watched her go out the drive and climb into her gay little coupé, and then and there I swore to sever my connection with the police after this case was over. It was dirty work. I did their dirty work for them. What was I but a stool pigeon, after all?

The police car moved forward as she got under way.

CHAPTER VIII

She had been gone less than an hour, and Hugo and Mary had not yet returned, when I heard a newsboy calling an extra. I went out to the street and bought one, and I saw that the verdict had been brought in: accidental death, and seemingly fair enough of course, with that gun laid out for cleaning and no powder marks found on the body.

Doctor Stewart came in soon afterward, brisk and cheerful, and he was the one who told Miss Juliet. She took it quietly, although I was watching for some sign. She merely sighed, and asked if Hugo and Mary had returned. It was Mr. Glenn, coming in at lunchtime, who explained the full significance of the verdict to her: that there would be considerable insurance. If he had expected her to show surprise, he was disappointed, although I thought she moved uneasily.

"Nothing can bring him back," he said, "so I can see no reason for not considering the change this makes in your circumstances." He had to repeat that, raising his voice, and she said nothing for an appreciable time. Then she raised herself on her elbow.

75

"So I keep my house after all!" she said. "On blood money!"

"I wouldn't look at it that way, Miss Juliet."

"What else is it?"

"It's a good many things; it is security and comfort in your old age. It means that you keep your home, the house which has stood for a great deal which is fine in this town for a good many years. That's something, isn't it? And these are hard times. Most of us are having our own troubles."

He drew a long breath, and she saw it rather than heard it.

"If I can help you, Arthur—"

"No, no," he said hastily. "I'm all right. I spend a lot, but then I make a lot!"

"Not from me," she said dryly.

He only smiled at that, and got up. As he looked down at her, his smile faded.

"One thing this ought to do, Miss Juliet," he said gravely. "It ought to reassure you about Herbert. It was an accident. Just remember that, and stop worrying."

I found myself wishing that the girl could have heard that conversation, and could have seen Miss Juliet's face. It was inconceivable that she could be acting for my benefit, or Mr. Glenn's. Yet even as I thought that, I was remembering that curious stealthy opening of the hall door the morning before. The door opening, and Miss Juliet slipping something under her pillow, hiding it from me.

I took my regular off-duty that afternoon, leaving Mary in the sickroom, and met the Inspector at his office at half past two.

"Well," he said, when I entered. "I suppose you saw the verdict? And thanks for the message. We've got the girl. That is, we know who she is, and we can lay our hands on her if we need her."

"Who is she?"

"Paula Brent."

"Paula Brent!"

He smiled at my astonishment. If the Mitchells had once been the leading family in the city, the Brents were now just that. With the usual difference, of course, that whereas no Mitchell ever allowed a picture in the paper or a reporter within a mile, the Brents were constantly featured. I thought fast. No wonder her family had objected to Herbert Wynne. The only wonder was that I had not recognized the girl. She had been a debutante the year before; I must have seen dozens of her photographs.

"It doesn't seem possible."

"That's what makes this business interesting. Nothing's impossible in it."

I was to remember that later.

He listened to her story attentively, as I told it. Here and there, he asked a question, and he made a note about the shattering of the windshield on her car.

"Easy to check that," he said.

But on the whole he was less impressed than I had thought he would be.

"We'll get her in and talk to her. But all she has, so far as I can see, is a dislike of the old lady that she has translated into suspicion. It's not as easy as all that. It does account for that suitcase, though. It's been bothering me."

He was more interested, apparently, in my account

77

of what had happened the night before, and particularly in my discovery of Hugo in the parlor.

"It's possible he saw someone, as he claims," he said thoughtfully. "On the other hand, it's always possible that he knows more than he's acknowledging. Remember, we're dealing with somebody who is no fool; that is, if this *is* a murder. And if it is supposed to be a murder by someone outside, what better proof that the house has been broken into once than to pretend that it's been done again? Still, if you saw the thing yourself, and are sure it wasn't simply nerves—"

"If I had any nerves of that sort," I said rather sharply, "I would certainly not take this work for you!"

"It was there, eh?"

"Something was. It was there, and then it wasn't."

"And it moved toward you?"

"It seemed to. I can tell you here and now, if I'd had a gun in my hand, I'd have shot it."

"And quite right, too," he said soothingly. "That's one reason I told you to leave your gun at home."

He leaned back in his chair, drew out his pipe and filled it thoughtfully.

"I gather that you found no ladder marks."

"None whatever."

"Well, think this over and see what you make of it. Between three and four on Tuesday morning, that would be three hours after the crime—if it was a crime—a man named Baird, who lives half a block from the Mitchell place, telephoned in to the precinct station nearby. He said that he was tending a sick dog in his garage, and that he had just seen a man enter the next property, which is the Manchester place, carrying a ladder. He had notified the people in the house, and they were investigating.

"A couple of men went around there, and they found the ladder all right. It was not where it had been left the night before, but it belonged to the Manchester place, right enough. In other words, somebody had carried that ladder away, used it for some purpose, and then brought it back."

"How long a ladder?"

"Long enough to reach to the roof of that ell on the Mitchell house."

"And then, I suppose, whoever it was flapped his wings and flew into the window above."

He laughed a little. "That's it," he said. "If that window was only above the roof we'd have something to go on. But it isn't. It's a good four feet to one side. But the time is interesting, isn't it? We got the body out at two, and I came back to talk to you at three, or something after three."

"Then that noise you heard—?"

"Possibly; although I'd hate to admit that while I sat on that front porch, somebody had put a ladder to that roof so that somebody else could get off it! If that ever got out, I'd be through, *finis!*"

"The sound I heard from the kitchen was earlier than that, of course," I said. "Did you get any description of this man?"

"Not much. Tall, and apparently strong, Baird says; he carried the ladder easily. He'd come across lots, avoiding the street. But here's an odd thing, although Baird is probably mistaken. He says that this fellow with the ladder wore a dinner jacket!

79

Baird couldn't see his face. The man had a soft hat, well pulled down, but he'll swear to the shirt front and so on. But why a ladder? I've looked at it, and if anybody could get into that third-floor window with it, he's a human fly; that's all."

"There were no ladder marks, anyhow."

"They could have been erased, of course."

I must have started, but he had walked to the window and was standing there with his back to me and did not notice.

"You see where we are," he said, still at the window. "This girl of yours has it all doped out. Those three elderly people did it, so Miss Juliet wouldn't have to go to the poorhouse! And old Hugo rented a car and followed him, so the boy began to carry a gun for self-defense! What sort of story did that lad invent to tell her, and why did he invent it?"

"It may just possibly be true."

"Possibly. But why should Hugo, having, we'll say, followed him for some time, and at least once fired at him outside, have chosen to shoot him in his own room, where, under the circumstances, he was bound to be suspected? Tell me that, Miss Pinkerton in the red hat. By the way, it's a nice hat."

"Thanks. I need a few kind words."

He laughed at that, and, coming back to his desk again, sat leaning back in his chair.

"Well, as I may have said before, it's the very devil of a case. We have only two alternatives: either the boy was putting up a front that night in order not to distress this girl, and then went home and killed himself. Which doesn't seem likely, if she's telling the truth. Or this fear of his had a sound basis, and he was killed. If he did it himself, how did he do it? If he didn't do it, then who did, and why, and how? That's the way it has to be, and here I am, with the whole Homicide Squad ready to go and no place to go. What's the use of tailing Hugo? To the grocery store and back again? And time is passing, and in crime it's the first hundred minutes that are the hardest—for the criminal. After that every hour helps him."

I asked him about the fingerprints on the gun, and I learned that the verdict at the inquest had largely been based on them.

"They're Herbert's, all right," he told me. "Smeared, but faintly readable. Of course the coroner knows, and I know, that that gun may have been held in a handkerchief, or fired through a pocket; or that the killer, if there was one, could have worn gloves. But a suicide usually freezes to the weapon until it's all over, and leaves a pretty clean print. Still, I don't mind telling you that if I could think of some method by which that lad could have shot himself in the forehead without leaving any contact marks, I'd go home and call it a day."

I did not remind him of the position of the body, or of that bullet mark on the fireplace. He knew all that better than I did, and he had no intention of calling it a day. That was shown by his next move, which was to open a drawer of his desk and fling out three photographs.

"Study these," he said. "Maybe you will see something I don't. I've looked at them until I can't see them any more."

I did not like them much, but a nurse has to see a good bit of death, one way and another, and so I took them to the window and inspected them carefully. One was a close-up of the body; another showed the body and the bureau; and a third, taken from the doorway, showed almost the entire room, including the fireplace. But the second one showed a small spot of white on the floor, between the body and the bureau, and I found myself staring at it. It was a roughly triangular bit of white, perhaps two inches across.

"See anything?" the Inspector inquired.

"No . . . but what's this bit of white on the floor? Is it a defect in the film?"

"A defect? Don't use that word where Johnny Nicholson can hear you. You'll break his heart!" He sauntered over and glanced at the picture in my hand. "Where?"

"There, a little underneath the bureau."

"It looks like a bit of paper," he said. "Why?"

"I don't know, I just wondered. I suppose—isn't that the *News* on the bureau?"

"It is. Our famous tabloid."

"But it was the *Eagle* he bought, according to Paula Brent. He bought the *Eagle* and looked at the financial page."

"That doesn't mean that he took it home with him. Still, I wouldn't mind seeing that paper. It's just possible—" He took the magnifying glass and inspected the picture again, with what I thought was a certain excitement. Evidently under the glass he saw something he had not seen before, for he turned to me abruptly.

"What became of that newspaper? Have you any idea?" he demanded.

"Not the slightest. The last time I saw it, the officer you had left with the body was reading it."

And then he blew up. "The infernal fool!" he shouted. "The double-distilled idiot! I'll break him for that. And somebody ought to break me! I don't belong on this job; I ought to be in a stable somewhere, being fed with a pitchfork. I suppose the room was cleared that night, after we took the body away?"

"Not until the next day; then you told them they could clean it. And they did."

"They would," he said grimly. "They knew, or guessed. Or maybe that was what Miss Juliet went after. She'd heard of it somehow. Damn Kelly. If that paper had been where I left it—"

Well, I knew the routine pretty well by that time, and that nothing should have been moved or touched. At the same time, the Squad had finished its work when Kelly took that paper; even the photographers had gone. And it is dreary work sitting up with a body, as well I know. But I said nothing, while the Inspector sat biting on an empty pipe and muttering to himself.

"What becomes of the papers from the Mitchell house?" he asked at last. "Are they saved?"

"Hugo burns them."

"He would!" he said viciously. "He'd burn that one, sure. And to think I never guessed it! I look all around for some sort of contrivance so he could kill himself and leave no powder marks; and there it lay, the simplest contrivance in the world. Look at that scrap on the floor. Does it suggest anything to you?"

"Not a thing."

"Well, you're not alone in that." His tone was still vicious. "It didn't suggest anything that night to a half-dozen bright young men whose job it was to find just such things."

"Are you trying to tell me that Herbert Wynne killed himself?"

"I think it's damned possible. And I think that that scrap on the floor should have told it to a lot of braying jackasses who were going around acting like detectives, including myself, if they'd had one good brain among the lot. There was a case like this in New England last spring. Probably Herbert saw it in the papers, and maybe the old lady saw it, too."

He picked up a newspaper, laid it flat on the top of the desk, but with a few inches hanging over the side, and then knelt in front of it.

"Now watch. I'm going to kill myself, but I carry a lot of insurance, so I want it to look like murder or an accident. Here's how it's done."

CHAPTER IX

He got out his fountain pen, and showed it to me. "Now see," he said. "This pen is my gun. I'm going to shoot myself with it, but I don't want any powder marks. So I lift two or three of the top pages of the paper out of the way; not too far. I want them to fall back later and cover the others. And I leave some of the bottom ones, too. Then I hold up these half dozen in the center. Do you get the idea?"

"I think so."

"Good. I'm going to shoot myself, but through these center pages. Then the powder marks will be on the paper, not on me. And as I let go and drop, the top pages will fall over and cover the others. Picked up and glanced at, that newspaper is all right. The front and back pages show nothing. I looked at that newspaper, and you say Kelly picked it up and read some of it. But the inside pages had a bullet hole through them just the same; and powder on them. And there was powder on that scrap, too, unless I'm crazy. It wasn't torn off; it was shot off. He was a smart boy, Miss Adams, and if I can prove how smart he was, I'd save the insurance companies a

85

lot of money."

"I don't believe it," I said stubbornly.

"Believe it or not, that's the way it looks. The chances are that that scrap wasn't on the floor at all when our fellows went over the place. It was loose, though, and the first flash dislodged it."

"And the cleaning rags and the oil, set out on the bureau?"

"Camouflage, Miss Pinkerton! Darned good camouflage, if I do say it."

I could only shake my head. "You talk to this girl," I told him. "I don't believe that that boy went to the movies that night, bought a paper to look at the financial page, kissed his sweetheart goodbye, told her to be ready to run away with him in a day or two, said that they would soon be sitting pretty, as he expressed it, and then went whistling down the street to kill himself. It's nonsense."

He looked slightly crestfallen. "You didn't tell me all that, before. I'll get her here, and get the truth out of her."

"She'll tell you just what she told me. Maybe he did kill himself, but he didn't expect to do it when he left her. He left her around eleven, and Miss Juliet found the body about twelve. That gave him less than an hour to get home and to have something happen which would lead him to kill himself. And where did he get that copy of the *News?* Don't tell me he stopped and bought it so he could use it as you say, when he had the *Eagle* in his pocket. You talk to Paula Brent, and then find whoever put that copy of the *Daily News* on that bureau. If it's possible to have a suicide arranged to look like a murder, why not a murder that looks like a suicide?"

"But it didn't look like a suicide. Remember that."

"Well, like accidental death. That's the verdict, isn't it? And here's another thing, Inspector. I don't believe he invented that story about being followed. And who shot at him, that night in the country? You'll find that that's true."

"Plenty of that going on these days," he retorted. "I still insist that if he meant to kill himself, and wanted it to be considered a murder, he would make up a story just like that, and tell it where it would be repeated."

"Why should he want it to be considered a murder? If he set that stage, as it was set, with the things for cleaning his gun all over the place, then he meant it to be considered an accident. If he meant anything at all."

And with that for him to think about, I went back to my patient.

I did not go directly back. I was annoyed with the Inspector and rather upset myself. For the first time in my experience I found not only my sympathy but my judgment opposed to that of Headquarters. I did not believe that Herbert Wynne had killed himself. I believed Paula Brent's story, vague as it was, and I dreaded the ordeal of interrogation which I knew was before her.

I was undecided when I reached the street. I called a taxicab, and stood with my hand on the door, still hesitating. Then I gave the address of the Brent house in Rosedale, crawled in, and gave myself up to an emotional orgy of irresolution and remorse. I was on my way to warn Paula. I knew police methods. Who better? They would not use physical force with her, of course, but they would discover at once that she was not telling all she knew. After that, they would not stop. They would keep after her, poor little thing; firing questions at her until she was exhausted, playing tricks on her, waiting until she was utterly weary and then pouncing.

I was pretty much exhausted myself when I got to Rosedale. Once a suburb, it is now a part of the city, and I knew the Brent house by sight. It was one of those large brick Colonial houses which should be set back among trees, and instead took up almost all of the lot. At the rear was a garage, and behind that an alley. The block was almost solidly built up, and the alley on both sides lined with similar garages, brick and frame.

Paula was at home, and her mother out. This last was no surprise to me. Mrs. Brent was on the Woman's Board of St. Luke's, and when she was not there, running her finger around for dust and prying into the refrigerators in the diet kitchens, she was somewhere else doing the same thing. I knew the type; the sort who leaves her daughter to a governess until she is old enough to come out, and then wonders why she gets into trouble.

The butler showed me into a large living room, and I found Paula there. She had apparently been curled up in the corner of a davenport until I came in, and I had a feeling that she had not been alone there; that someone had left the room by a rear door as I entered. I thought she looked somewhat better, and she even managed a smile, although I saw that she was startled.

88

"Then you knew me, all along," she said.

I had not thought of that, and it took some quick thinking. "I've seen a good many pictures of you, Miss Brent."

"Funny! I never thought of that."

But when I told her that the police would probably want to ask her some questions, she sat down suddenly, as though she had gone weak in the knees.

"What makes you think that?"

"They saw you with me this morning, and I think they followed you home," I said shamelessly. "I thought maybe I'd better tell you. They have a way of getting the facts, you know."

She lighted a cigarette, and I thought her hands were unsteady. But she looked at me again with that queer look of defiance that I had noticed before.

"I'll tell them just what I told you."

"If there is anything else—"

"There is nothing else. Herbert was killed by someone in that house, probably Hugo, and that old woman knows it. If the police are out to whitewash the Mitchell family, I'll call in a bunch of reporters and tell them so! You can tell them that, if you like."

But it was bravado. So was the cigarette, and her whole general attitude. She was very pale, and the next thing I knew, she was crumpled up in a heap on the davenport, crying as though her heart would break. I found myself trying to quiet her, and from that moment on, through all that was on the way for all of us, I found myself unconsciously on that child's side, and against the police.

And that in spite of the fact that I was fully aware, as the butler showed me out, that she had already

89

started back for that rear door, where somebody unknown had been waiting and probably listening.

Miss Juliet ate a fair supper that evening, and I must say that everybody around the place seemed more cheerful than I had yet seen them. The meal, too, was the most substantial I had seen served, and Hugo moved almost lightly around the table. After all, why not? No one there had had any affection for Herbert Wynne, and his passing and the verdict meant a clear hundred thousand dollars for them. I began to think, not that the death had been as the Inspector now believed, but that it had had its compensations. After all, comfort and security for the old age of three elderly people were not such bad things in exchange for a boy who had obviously been of little value to the world, save to one girl, who would soon forget him.

I was, however, rather surprised to learn that certain plans had been made in my absence. Hugo told me of them when he brought in my dessert.

"I beg pardon, miss, but I thought you would like to know. Doctor Stewart and Mr. Glenn are going to be in the house tonight."

"Both of them? What for?"

"The gentlemen consider it advisable, miss. Mr. Glenn will be here until two o'clock, and Doctor Stewart will spend the remainder of the night. I understand that he has a case which will keep him until about that time."

"They haven't said why?"

"No, miss."

90

I lost patience at that. "Now listen to me, Hugo. If you know anything, it's your business to tell the police. What is it? Who was here last night, on that landing? And who are they afraid will get in again tonight?"

But he had no explanation beyond what I already knew. The two men had met there late that afternoon, and Hugo had told them about the night before. It was Mr. Glenn who had suggested the watch on the house.

"After all, miss," Hugo went on, "if somebody got in on Monday night and again last night, there's no telling when they will try again."

"But for what purpose, Hugo? Why should somebody try to get in?"

"I haven't any idea, miss."

And somehow I believed him.

Nevertheless there was an element of humor in that night's vigil as kept by the two men who had arranged it, and also a bit of drama. One or two small things, too, rather roused my curiosity.

Thus, although the general atmosphere had certainly improved, I thought there was some sort of trouble between Mary and Hugo that evening. She stood sullenly over her stove while Hugo prepared Miss Juliet's tray, and once, when he spoke to her, she ignored him. Also, while she relieved me for my dinner, she must have said something to the old lady which upset her, for her pulse was faster when I went back to her.

Some of the humor lay in Mr. Glenn's rather ponderous and meticulous examination of the house when he arrived at nine o'clock. He spent some time

91

in the kitchen with Mary, and then proceeded to go over the entire place, including the cellars; and the only good laugh I had during that entire week was when he somehow managed to knock over a can of red paint at the top of the cellar stairs, slip on the top step, and bump all the way to the bottom.

He was not hurt, but he was outraged to the very depths of his soul. I could hear him swearing clear up in the sickroom, and I was just in time to see him emerging, apparently covered with blood, and in a vicious humor. He had to send home for other clothes, and the house smelled of paint all night!

Mary was sullenly viewing the wreckage when I went back again.

"How on earth did he do it, Mary?"

"I don't know, miss. He'd do well to keep to his own part of the house. That's all."

After that we settled down. Apparently Mr. Glenn had brought some work with him, for at ten o'clock his confidential secretary arrived, and as it turned out, it was she—her name, I learned later, was Florence Lenz—who provided the only bit of drama we had that Wednesday night.

I had seen her when she came in, and I did not like her much. She had evidently made a special toilet for the occasion, and she stopped in the hall to powder her nose. I knew her sort the minute I saw her. They never forget that their employer is a man, and when he is, like Mr. Glenn, pretty much a man of the world and not married, that he may represent anything from a tidy flat to a marriage license.

But she was evidently an efficient secretary, and they worked together in the library with the door open until midnight. Now and then he would emerge, make a round of the lower floor, and then go back again. I could hear his voice, monotonously dictating something to her, and only broken by these tours of duty.

Then, at twelve o'clock, he let her go, sending her out to his car and calling to the chauffeur to take her home. And it was not more than three minutes later, when I had at last settled down for some sleep, that I heard the doorbell ringing furiously and Mr. Glenn running to the door.

I was a trifle scared myself when he opened it. There was the chauffeur with the secretary in his arms. Looking as helpless as men always do at such times.

"What's the matter? Is she hurt?"

And with that she released herself, stumbled through the doorway and dropped gracefully on the floor at Mr. Glenn's feet! I ran down at once, in my dressing gown and bare feet, and I had only to touch her eyeballs to know that she was no more in a faint than I was. It did not take me long to go back to the kitchen and get a bottle of household ammonia. I had seen plenty of this fake fainting, and I have never known anything quicker than a good whiff of that stuff to bring them around.

It did not take her long. She choked and coughed, and when she opened her eyes, she gave me a look of plain hatred! But she came around all right, and it turned out that she had something to tell after all. I had not believed it at first, nor, I think, had Mr. Glenn.

"Sit up, Miss Lenz, and don't be an idiot," he said.

93

"What's the matter? What happened to you?"

"A man," she said, still coughing from the ammonia. "A man. He knocked me down and ran over me."

"*Knocked* you down? He attacked you?"

"He knocked me down and ran over me."

"You've said that before! Where was all this?"

"Around the corner."

"What corner?"

"Around the corner of the house."

And there was certainly some truth in what she claimed, as we realized when we looked at her. Her knee was cut—she wore her stockings rolled, of course!—and she had a considerable bump on her head. Mr. Glenn asked no more questions. He went out the front door in a hurry, leaving Florence glaring at me.

"That's a dirty trick you pulled!" she said.

"It revived you."

"It damn near killed me."

Well, there was enough truth in that to send me rather remorsefully upstairs for some dressings and adhesive plaster. I was still working over her knee, and she was making a lot of fuss about it, when Mr. Glenn came back and she told her story.

She had started for the car, and then decided to go around the house and take what she elegantly called a look-see. All her life she had heard of the Mitchell place, and now she was inside the gates.

"I told Mac to wait," she said—Mac was evidently Mr. Glenn's chauffeur—"and that I was going to walk around the house. But as I rounded the corner at the back, this fellow bumped into me, and how!

Well, he knocked me flat, but did he stop? He did not. He simply jumped over me and beat it. You can ask Mac. He heard him running."

Well, it might or might not be important. I didn't know. We got rid of her at last, loudly calling on "Mac" to bear her out, and limping so that Mr. Glenn had to help her to the car. But that was the only dramatic incident of the night. When the doctor arrived at two o'clock, his reaction to the Lenz girl's story was characteristic.

"Somebody's chauffeur, going home late across lots," he said dryly. "Probably worse scared than the girl, at that."

And I gathered, after the lawyer had left, that the doctor considered the whole idea a silly one.

"I'm ready to do my bit," he said to me. "I'm used to losing sleep, if it comes to that. But what the hell do Glenn and Hugo think anyone wants out of this house? A lot of secondhand furniture?"

After which he proceeded to settle himself on the old sofa in the hall, and to sleep there comfortably for the rest of the night. I could hear him snoring as I lay on my extemporized bed at the foot of the big walnut one, so I finally dropped off myself. I needed sleep that night, and I got it.

CHAPTER X

That was on Wednesday night.

I wakened early the next morning, and lay on my sofa, thinking over the newspaper incident and the Inspector's theory about it. It seemed to me, not only that if a suicide could be planned to look like a murder, a murder could also be planned to look like a suicide; but that in this latter event the newspaper became extremely important. For suppose a charge of murder was made, against Hugo, for example? What would be simpler than for Hugo to produce that paper and thus demonstrate that Herbert had killed himself, but had carefully arranged it to look like murder or accidental death?

In that case the paper would not have been destroyed. It would be carefully hidden, perhaps somewhere in the library, where I had missed it, or better still, in that back flat where Hugo and Mary lived their silent lives together.

At seven o'clock I heard Doctor Stewart moving in the hall below. There was an old-fashioned marble washstand built in under the stairs, and I could hear him washing there. Soon after that he went outside,

97

and I could see him from a window making a round of the house. Apparently he discovered nothing suspicious there, for when he had had a cup of coffee, he came up to see Miss Juliet, and he was scornful about the whole business.

"I don't believe there was anyone there at all," he said. "What I think is that that girl, whatever her name is, fell over something and then cooked up a story for Glenn. Makes her interesting! And Glenn's not married."

He left soon after that, and I went down to get my own breakfast. But I found myself watching Hugo that morning with a sort of indignation. What manner of man was this, if I were right, putting down my coffee with a steady hand, bringing in my bacon, and placing the morning paper before me almost with a flourish: "WYNNE VERDICT—ACCIDENTAL DEATH." I looked up and caught his eye, and I thought he looked away.

"So they've settled it, Hugo!"

"It's all settled, miss. Apparently."

But for all his flourish, he seemed quiet and depressed. There was no talk going on in the kitchen when I got the old lady's tray, and Mary was still sullen and morose.

Just what was it that Mary knew, and Miss Juliet? For that they shared some guilty knowledge I felt convinced by that time. Why must Mary write her messages to the old lady and then destroy them? Why had she resented Mr. Glenn the night before?

I have lain awake at night since, wondering if poor old Miss Juliet ever felt that I suspected her of some tacit connivance in that crime, and thinking of the

98

price she had to pay to convince me that she was innocent. Poor old Miss Juliet Mitchell, succumbing to her one moment of temptation, and so sending herself in all innocence to what the Inspector called the black-out! I was glad that she never knew that. And I am glad to remember that if, from that time on, there was little kindness in my care of her, at least I did my duty by her. And I hope a little more.

They buried Herbert that morning, Thursday, from a mortuary chapel in the town. I gathered later that there was a small attendance of old friends of the family, and an enormous crowd of morbid-minded people there. And that at least one person attended in simple grief and with utter recklessness of consequences—Paula Brent. Hugo did not go at all, but at ten o'clock Mary appeared in the doorway of Miss Juliet's room, clad in the black raiment which certain people keep for such occasions, and shouted to the old lady.

"I'm going, Miss Juliet."

"Thank you, Mary."

That was all.

At noon the Inspector called me up, to say that he was going to talk to Paula Brent that afternoon, and would like me to be there.

"You'd better come down and check on her story," he said. "Watch out for any discrepancies. She's pretty much haywire just now, but she'll have settled down by the time you get here."

I looked about, but Hugo was in the kitchen, and Mary had not come back. I lowered my voice. "You might have given her a little time, after this morning!"

"She's had three days," he said, rather ominously, and hung up the receiver.

I was considerably upset when I went upstairs again. What did he mean by that three days?

Mary came back soon afterward, and when I went upstairs after lunch, I found that she had been carrying down the dead boy's clothes, and piling them on the stairs to the third floor. They lay outside Miss Juliet's room, on the lower steps, piled in neat bundles; his shirts, his collars and ties, his suits of clothing. There was something dreadful to me in that haste of hers to get rid of the last vestiges of that unlucky youth, and I called Mary into the hall and said so.

"What is the hurry?" I asked. "That could wait, couldn't it?"

"It was her idea," she said sourly. "She wants to look them over. They're to go to the Salvation Army. And what's wrong about it? He'll never need them again."

When I went in, I found Miss Juliet's pulse fast again, and not too good. I gave her some digitalis, and I advised her to let the clothing wait for a day or two.

"You're in no condition to do things like that, Miss Juliet," I told her sternly. "A day won't matter, and I won't be answerable to the doctor if you don't obey orders."

She nodded. "Mary wanted to get them out of the house," she said. "Certainly there is no hurry."

Well, I could make what I wanted of those two statements, Mary's and hers, although I was pretty much puzzled. Had they been going over his clothing

100

together, those two old women, searching for something? I thought of that as she nibbled without appetite at the food on the tray I had carried up. Were they afraid he had left something, a letter perhaps, which would weaken or destroy the verdict which meant so much to them? A letter was the usual thing left by suicides.

Still, if he had killed himself, why take all that trouble to make it look like something else, and then leave such a letter? Unless it was a letter he might have received, from Paula perhaps. Almost certainly she would have written to him.

The only thing I could work out from that was that Paula might have written him something about the danger he was in, and that those two women suspected that she had. But, of course, that implied that they knew both of this danger and about Paula. I was not sure that they knew either. Actually I was sure of only one thing, and that was that they had made a systematic search of the dead boy's clothing.

That theory was verified when I saw that the coat which Mary had hastily laid on the stairs as I appeared had a pocket turned inside out. Of course that really proved nothing. Everyone goes over clothing before giving it away. Or the police might have done it. It was only the haste and stealth of the performance that looked queer to me.

I would rather have had a tooth pulled than go into the Inspector's neat and tidy office that afternoon. Unlike the Police Commissioner's room, which was a sort of murder museum with revolvers, dirks and even a bit of charred human bone glued to a card, the Inspector's office was bare to the last degree. A chair

101

or two, a big desk, and two telephones were all that it contained. But I stood for some time with my hand on the knob of the door, before I could make up my mind to go in and face Paula Brent. Nor was my discomfort lessened when she looked up at me with a dreary little smile.

"So they've got you, too!" she said.

"It looks like it."

"Well, I hope he believes you. He doesn't believe me. He thinks Herbert killed himself."

"If he was sure of that, you wouldn't be here," I told her.

And that turned out to be the case. The interrogation had barely commenced, but I saw at once that the Inspector had at least temporarily abandoned the suicide theory.

She bore up under it very well, although watching her as she sat in her straight chair—facing the light, as did everyone called for questioning into that office—I saw what struck me as rather pathetic; that she had put on a black dress and a little black hat for the funeral.

It had its effect on the Inspector also, for he handled her with rather unusual gentleness. And I must say that the story she told him was the story she had told me, word for word. Now and then he looked at me, and I nodded. It was not until he began to question her that she seemed less assured.

"Now, about your being on the Mitchell place that night. You hadn't, by any chance, been in the house with him?"

"What do you mean by that?"

"I'm asking you, Miss Brent. Don't get the idea

102

that I think you killed him. I know better. But if you had quarreled, and after you left, he had decided to— you see what I mean."

"Never. We had never quarreled."

"Tell me about the two hours between the time you separated, and the time you saw the house lighted and a police car in the drive."

"I just drove around," she said vaguely. "I was nervous."

"Drove for two hours? Where did you go?"

"I really don't know."

"You must know," he said sharply. "You know the roads around here. You had to get back home. Come, come, Miss Brent! Don't you want us to learn the truth about all this?"

"What I did has nothing to do with that. I didn't kill him."

"Well, where were you when you had the trouble, on what road?"

"Trouble? What sort of trouble?"

"Didn't something happen to your car?"

She remembered then, and glanced at me suspiciously. "I had a flat tire. It was outside of Norrisville. It took me a good while to change it."

And then, while she was still confused over that temporary lapse, he flung a bomb at her.

"Just why did you get that ladder?"

She stared at him, her lips slightly parted. For a moment she could not speak.

"I don't know what you mean by a ladder."

"I think you do," he said quietly. "And I warn you against concealing anything which has a bearing on this case. You got a ladder and dragged it across

103

two lawns and through the shrubbery of the Mitchell place; and a good trail you left. If you want to see it, I have a rough drawing here."

But she made no move to look at it. She sat huddled in her chair, her face white and drawn. "I don't understand," she said weakly. "I don't know what you're talking about."

Nor did I, for that matter. The afternoon before, he had told me that a man had carried that ladder, and now here he was accusing this girl. He has his own methods, however, and in the next question he had apparently abandoned the ladder, and shifted to something else.

"You told Miss Adams that Herbert's family, or rather Miss Mitchell and her household, did not like him."

"They hated him."

"How do you know that?"

"He always said so. Lately it had been worse. For a month or so."

"What do you mean by worse?"

"He got frightened. They were following him."

"That's rather absurd, isn't it? Old Miss Juliet could follow nobody."

"Somebody was following him. He began to carry his revolver."

"He never said who it was?"

"He didn't know. I think now that it was Hugo."

"Why Hugo?"

I need not repeat that part of her story. It was much like what she had told me. But she added something which was new. This was to the effect that, while Herbert had refused to explain his fears and suspicions to her, he had told her he had written a letter, so that if anything happened to him, she would understand. And that on Wednesday morning, when I had surprised her in the yard, she had been trying to get into the house to find it.

"That's the truth, is it?"

"I've told you."

"You weren't there to see if that ladder had left any marks, and to erase them if you found them?"

"What ladder?"

But the questions had evidently alarmed her, for now she began to cry. She didn't know anything about a ladder. She wished he would let her alone. She wanted to go home. After all, she hadn't killed Herbert, although the Inspector acted as though she had. When she was quieter, I noticed that he had tactfully abandoned the ladder.

"This letter you speak of, did he tell anyone else about it?"

"He wouldn't. I'm sure he never did."

He nodded, and shortly after that he got up.

"You understand, of course, that you re not under arrest. That would be ridiculous. But I shall ask you a few more questions, and I'll see that your family is notified of your safety. You'll be home tonight, all right. In the meantime the matron will see that you are comfortable, and we'll have some food sent in."

"Why not ask them now?" she said. "If I'm not guilty, you have no business to hold me."

"Maybe not." He smiled down at her. "But I can't ask my questions yet; and after all, you and I want the same thing, don't we? We want to know who killed Herbert Wynne, if he was killed. And why."

CHAPTER XI

She went, chin high and her bearing faintly defiant, when the matron came. The Inspector followed her out with his eyes, and waited until the door had closed.

"How about it, Miss Adams?"

"It's the same story."

"She almost forgot the tire!"

"That doesn't prove anything, does it? She has had a lot to distract her. How on earth did you learn that she had dragged that ladder, Inspector?"

"I didn't," he said calmly. "We found the tracks, all right. They led toward the Mitchell house. But we found none leading back. In other words, it looked as though someone without strength to carry it had taken it to the house; that might be a woman, or a girl. But it had been carried back; somebody had had strength enough to do that, and as you know, this man was seen."

"And that footprint was hers?"

"That's my guess. She wore high heels, and so she slipped off her pumps. She's intelligent, and if she was scared that night, she was still using her brains."

"Then you think she got somebody off that roof? On Monday night?"

"I do indeed, Miss Pinkerton!"

"Who?"

But he ignored that for the time. He got out his old briar pipe and carefully filled it.

"It's like this," he said finally. "When there's a question between murder and suicide, we have only one choice. We have to go on the murder theory until that's disproved. That doesn't mean that it is a murder. It only means that it may be a murder. But in this case there are a number of things that begin to confirm my first impressions. The coroner didn't have all of them. I can't see that boy in front of the bureau when that shot was fired, and I know he didn't move a foot after it *was* fired. But I can't see that ladder either, unless it was used to let somebody escape from that roof who had no business to be there. Any more than this fellow in the grounds had any business there last night."

"You know about that, do you?" I asked, surprised.

"I know a little about a lot of things," he said. "And not enough about any one of them. For instance, why the deuce let those two amateur sleuths take over the job of the police?"

"It was their idea, not mine. I'd told you I had seen something on the landing the night before," I said indignantly. "But you were too busy shooting yourself through a newspaper to pay much attention."

He grinned at that, but he was sober enough as he went on. "Well, we both slipped up there," he

108

agreed. "The point is that Hugo was scared last night, and that he didn't want the police. So he gets the two men he trusts; and we lose something that might be important."

He filled his pipe and leaned back in his chair. "After talking with this girl," he said, "I notice that there is one element which she has been mighty careful to keep out of her story. That's her family. She's frightened, and so she emphasizes the fact the Mitchell household disliked him.

"But somebody else may have had more than dislike for him. He was a weakling, with the unbridled passions of his type, and here was a nice girl in love with him. Who had a reason for putting him out of the way? Maybe more of a reason than we know?"

"I suppose you mean Mr. Brent. But I don't think—"

"No? Well, fathers have a way of looking after their daughters. And remember, this boy was a bad actor. He may already have—well, let's not get carried away. She looks like a girl with character, but just the same she has a father; and it's pretty certain that that father was afraid of him, and of what might happen. Mind you, I'm not accusing the father. He just enters the picture as a possibility, provided this turns out to be a murder.

"Now go back to that night. Herbert Wynne may have killed himself, but he was a fellow with a weak chin and that sort are pretty careful of their skins! Also, if she is right about his whistling when he left her and all that, we have to suppose that something happened between eleven and twelve o'clock that

109

night which changed his cheerfulness into despair. That's a pretty short time. What had he done, or what had he learned, to effect that change? Had Paula thrown him over? She doesn't act as though she had."

"She hadn't," I said positively. "Whether she was in love with him or simply infatuated, I don't know. But she's still wearing his ring, if you noticed."

He nodded. "I did notice. Nice ring, too. I'd like to know where he got the money for it . . . But let's get on to Mr. Brent again. And by the way, that story of the broken windshield is true enough. We've checked it."

"So Mr. Brent drove past his daughter's car, and fired at it! How did he know he wouldn't kill her?"

That annoyed him, although he laughed. "I've said that there is a good bit of indiscriminate shooting going on just now. Let's leave that for a minute. Suppose that the girl's father has followed them, seen them in the movies, and when the girl drove off, has followed him home. He goes in with him, there's a quarrel, the boy's revolver is on the table, and—because it has turned out that he deserves it—the father shoots him. Probably he didn't mean to, but there's the boy's gun on the bureau. Perhaps it was that shot that aroused Miss Juliet, although she doesn't know it. She opens her door, sees a light above, and starts up the stairs. The father is there, trapped!

"What does he do? He only has a few minutes. He drags the body in front of the bureau, bends the knees, and—using his handkerchief, of course—he puts the revolver on the floor beside him. Then he escapes, by the only way possible."

"By the window?"

"By the window. I believe a strong man could swing over to that roof of the ell, and do it safely. And now take the rest of the story. The girl watches those two go off, either together or the one following the other; and she knows there may be trouble. What does she do? She follows them and hangs around outside the house. That story about a flat tire near Norrisville is pure invention. She hangs around the Mitchell place, and she's not deaf, or asleep. She hears a shot fired.

"What can she do? She sees the lights going on, and knows that the household is alarmed and up. But so far as she knows, Mr. Brent is still in the building. She sees the police go in, and later on a Headquarters car. She still hangs around. She stops you, but you can't tell her anything. And she has to know, somehow.

"Now we get to the ladder. We'll say that Mr. Brent is on that roof. He can't get down, and he's gone if he's found there. It isn't hard to imagine that he saw her below and signaled to her, or that she waited until we had gone and then got that ladder. Of course, this is only conjecture, but something like that happened Monday night, if there was any murder at all."

"And so on Wednesday morning," I said, "when she knew that the servants were at the inquest, she went back there to—"

"Precisely. To look for the ladder marks and to erase them. You surprised her, and so she told you that story."

I sat for some time, thinking this over. It fitted

111

together too well to be ignored, but I was not certain of one or two things.

"He didn't go in with Herbert," I said at last. "Herbert had started to undress."

"Then he followed him later."

"How did he get in? The doorbell rings in the servants' bedroom as well as in the kitchen. It would have wakened them."

"He might have called, or thrown gravel. You and I know that that can be done."

But I was not satisfied. "Herbert wouldn't have admitted Mr. Brent," I said. "Not if Paula's story is true. He'd have known that it meant trouble."

But he only shrugged his shoulders. "One thing will happen if I'm right," he said. "We'll let the family know where Paula is, and if there is anything to this idea, he'll burst in as soon as he hears it. He'll probably do that anyhow," he added ruefully.

He let me go soon after that, merely saying that he would probably come up that night, to look over the roof and the window sill of Herbert's room.

"If this was a murder, then somebody was on that roof all the time we were examining the body and the room," he said. "As a matter of fact, I looked out over the roof myself. But there's a sizeable chimney there, and whoever it was, Brent or someone unknown, may have been behind it. But this girl knows who it was. You can bank on that.

"And don't forget this," he added, as I started to go. "That theory doesn't apply only to Brent. It applies to anyone who was interested in the girl."

It was four o'clock when I left the office, and four thirty when I got to the Mitchell place. I bought an evening paper on the way, and I saw that the press already knew that Paula Brent had been interrogated. "SOCIETY GIRL QUERIED IN MITCHELL CASE," was the heading. Following as it did on a coroner's verdict of accidental death, the *Eagle* had certainly made the most of it.

I was not surprised when I saw the doctor's car in the drive, but I was startled at Hugo's face when he let me in.

"She's had a bad turn, miss," he said. "The doctor's asking for you."

I went in, without changing my uniform, to find Miss Juliet lying back on her pillows, and both the doctor and Mary bending over her. The doctor was holding a towel to her nose, and the pungent odor of amyl-nitrite filled the room. When I took her wrist, her pulse was very rapid, and I noticed that her sallow face was flushed.

It was a full ten minutes before the doctor straightened and gave me the towel. "I think she'll do now," he said. "Did anything happen to cause this, Mary?"

"I don't know, doctor. She had been quiet enough. I had got her the paper and her reading glasses. Then I heard her give a quick breath, and let the paper drop. I called Hugo, and he called you."

Doctor Stewart stayed until almost seven. By that time Miss Juliet was better, but far from being herself. Most of the time she lay with her eyes closed, not speaking, although she was perfectly conscious; and she refused to take any nourishment whatever. It was only when the doctor was about to leave that she opened her eyes and said a few words.

113

"I want to see Arthur Glenn."

"Not tonight, Miss Juliet. Tomorrow will do, won't it?"

She nodded and closed her eyes again.

I followed the doctor into the hall, and he stood for a few minutes, apparently thinking hard.

"I'm not quite satisfied with the look of things, Miss Adams," he said. "It seems to me—did you notice the *Eagle* on the bed? I have an idea that what sent her off was an article stating that a young woman named Brent had been held for questioning by the police on this case."

"I saw that," I agreed cautiously.

"Well, that's understandable. The girl's grandfather had been a lover of Miss Juliet's years ago. Of course he is dead now, but it must have been a shock. Quite aside from that, however, is the fact that the police are interrogating anybody, after the coroner's verdict."

"I suppose they are not satisfied, doctor."

He eyed me impatiently. "That's a mild way of putting it, anyhow! What the hell do you think I'm talking about? Of course they're not satisfied. What I want you to do is to keep any suspicion of that away from the old lady. Let the police get themselves in the newspapers if they like. Miss Mitchell is an old woman with a bad heart. It may quit on her at any time. I don't want any more shocks for her; that's all."

He turned to go down the stairs, then turned back again. "Has she said anything about making a will?"

"Not to me, doctor."

"She may. She's worth money now. There's an old

114

one somewhere, with legacies for Mary and Hugo in it. Pretty substantial ones, I imagine. But if the will question comes up, let me know, will you? I might get some money for St. Luke's."

Well, I suppose that was natural enough. He had got a good bit of money for St. Luke's, one way and another. But I felt rather resentful as he went down the stairs. I made up my mind to keep my own counsel if the will question came up, and I was unusually tender with Miss Juliet that evening.

I was thoughtful, too. So there were already substantial legacies for the servants!

CHAPTER XII

I had plenty to think of as I prepared Miss Juliet for the night, straightening her bed and once more rubbing her thin old back. I settled her early, for I knew that the Inspector was coming. And it was while I was folding up that copy of the *Eagle* and putting it away for later reading that something came into my mind. I have had this happen before; I can puzzle over a thing until I am in a state of utter confusion, give it up, and then suddenly have the answer leap into my mind without any apparent reason.

Yet there was a connection, in a way, I dare say. I straighten Miss Juliet's pillows, and remember that she had hidden something there. I put away the *Eagle,* and I remember that search in the library for what I was certain Mary had concealed there. And then I am reaching behind the books, finding a dirty scrap of newspaper and leaving it there.

My first impulse was to go down at once and look for it. Hugo, however, was still on the lower floor, and I decided to wait until the house was quiet; or perhaps until the Inspector arrived. One thing I have learned from the police, and that is never to take a risk by being in a hurry.

It was eight o'clock, and the Inspector had not yet arrived, when Miss Juliet roused from what I had hoped was a sleep, to ask me if I had telephoned to Mr. Glenn.

"Not yet," I said. "Won't the morning do?"

But she was insistent. He was to come in the morning, and to come prepared to take down something she had to say; so in the end I went down to the telephone and called him.

"What does she want?" he asked. "Have you any idea?"

"She's going to make a statement of some sort. This affair of the Brent girl seems to have upset her."

"A statement, eh? What on earth does she know that requires a statement? Have you any idea?"

"No. But she has had something on her mind ever since this thing happened. Something she thinks has a bearing on the case."

"I'll come around now," he said. "I'm on my way to the theater, and I'll stop in."

That satisfied Miss Juliet when I told her. She was excited, I thought, and somehow I got the impression that she was frightened also; that she had determined to do something which she was afraid to do. I was standing at the window, watching for the lights of Mr. Glenn's car, when she spoke to me.

"I used to know Paula Brent's grandfather," she said, in her flat voice. "Why should they question Paula? She couldn't know anything about Herbert."

"I wouldn't let that bother you," I said, as gently as I could while shouting at her. "They've questioned a

118

lot of people."

"Why? If they think it was an accident?"

"Well, you know how these things are. The insurance company wants to be certain. That's all."

"Certain of what?"

I hesitated, but I had gone too far. She was watching me, and to save my life I could not think of any evasion.

"Of course it's nonsense, Miss Mitchell. They simply want to be certain that he—that it didn't happen by design."

"That he didn't kill himself?"

"Yes."

She closed her eyes, and although it was difficult to be sure in the dim light, I thought I saw tears oozing from beneath her wrinkled lids. But the next moment she apparently felt what I had not even heard, the vibration of Mr. Glenn's heavy car in the drive, and she visibly braced herself.

"There is Arthur," she said. "Will you tell him to come up? And then will you go out, my dear, so that I can talk to him?"

I did not go far; only into my room, which adjoined hers. But I could hear nothing after her first words. To tell the truth, I did not care to. Long ago I had made my position clear to the Inspector, that I was no eavesdropper, listening with my ear to a keyhole. I left them there, Mr. Glenn large and resplendent in dinner clothes, with two black pearl studs and a carefully tied black tie, and that frail old creature on the bed. Perhaps she did not realize that I had not yet closed the door when she spoke to him.

"Arthur," she said. "I have connived at a great

wickedness, and now I am going to save my soul."

It was then that he followed me to the door and closed it behind me.

He must have been very late for the theater that night. The conference lasted about a half hour; if one can call a conference what sounded like expostulation from him, and a monotonous sort of insistence from that walnut bed. Whatever she wanted to do, he was opposed to it. Once or twice, indeed, he raised his voice so that I actually heard what he said.

"I don't believe it," he said. "I don't care what he told you. I don't believe it."

And again: "You've had a bit of good fortune when you needed it. And if you'll look back, you'll see that it was coming to you."

But I doubt if his arguments had any effect whatever on her. At something before nine he went downstairs and out to the kitchen, and I heard Hugo calling up the back stairs to Mary, telling her to come down. Evidently she refused, and soon after, I heard Mr. Glenn banging out of the front door and driving away in his car.

When I went back to Miss Juliet, she was looking tired, but happier than I had seen her since I came.

"I feel much better, my dear," she said quietly. "Now I think I shall sleep."

And sleep she did, for at least part of a night which was to be filled with horror for me.

The Inspector did not arrive until half past nine, but I had no opportunity to get into the library during that interval. Hugo was prowling about the lower floor, now in the long parlor, now in the library. He looked disturbed and anxious, as well he

120

might be if my idea of Miss Juliet's talk with Mr. Glenn that night was correct. And as I sat in that dim room and checked it over, I myself could find no flaw in it.

I had a complete picture in my mind by that time; of Miss Juliet's salvaging that copy of the *News* from wherever Kelly had left it, and of finding the scrap on the floor and placing it inside. Almost certainly the scrap had still been inside when Mary got it and hid it, but when the paper was next moved, it had dropped out behind the books, and it had not been missed.

Then, if that were true, there had been no murder. Herbert Wynne had killed himself, and Miss Juliet's crime had consisted of withholding that knowledge. "I don't care what he told you," Mr. Glenn had said. What could that be but a reference to a possible method for making a suicide look like something else? And, although, as it turned out, I was entirely wrong in a good many things relating to this case, in that, at least, I was correct. Miss Juliet did know about that newspaper device.

At nine thirty the Inspector arrived, bringing a deputy inspector with him. I heard the three men, Hugo in the lead, going to the third floor, and after some considerable time I gathered that the deputy was on the roof of the rear wing, and that they were having trouble getting him off it.

I slipped into the hall and listened.

"All right, Evans," the Inspector was calling. "We'll get a ladder."

I had only time to slip back when the Inspector and Hugo came down the stairs. The Inspector was talking.

"There must be one in the neighborhood. A pruning ladder would do."

And Hugo's voice, quiet and respectful: "I believe the Manchesters have one, sir. That's quite a little distance, however."

"I guess we can manage it."

So Hugo knew of that ladder! I sat on the stairs and tried to think that out, until by the sounds outside I gathered that the two men had started for the Manchester place. Then, still confused, I slipped into the library. Confused, because once again the Inspector and I had shifted opinions on the case. That night, searching behind the books for that scrap of paper, I was as convinced as though I had been present that Herbert Wynne had shot himself; and at the same time the Inspector had veered once more to murder, and was out hunting a ladder to prove it.

So absorbed was I that I did not hear the men returning. I was having some difficulty in locating the scrap again; indeed, at first I was certain that it had been removed, and it was necessary to take out certain books and pile them on the floor before I found it. But at one glance I was satisfied. It was not only the proper size and shape, but it was scorched and stained with powder.

I had just tucked it into the waistband of my apron when I heard a sound in the hall, and turned to see Hugo in the doorway. His face gave me a very real shock, for if ever I have seen uncontrolled rage in a human countenance it was in his. He could not even speak for a perceptible time, and then it was an effort.

"What are you looking for, miss?"

122

"For a book to read," I said shortly.

He had regained control of himself by that time, and his voice was more civil. "If you have found one, I'll wait and put out the light."

"This will do," I said, and took one at random. It was only later on that I found it to be a highly technical discussion of ancient Greek art, and with it under my arm I marched out. I do not believe that his eyes left me for a second, from the time he discovered me until I turned the bend at the top of the stairs. Then, listening, I heard him go outside again, and I gathered that the unlucky deputy inspector was being rescued. Apparently he and Hugo returned the ladder, for the Inspector came back into the house and took advantage of that chance to talk to me.

"We're right so far," he said cheerfully. "Somebody got out of that window Monday night. Hung by his hands and swung over to the roof."

"You mean that you found prints?" I asked incredulously.

"They're there, but they're not clearly readable. As he swung before he let go, he smeared them all over the place. Still, we've learned that much."

But when I gave him the scrap of paper, he looked rather crestfallen.

"Powder stains, all right," he commented. "Well, your guess is as good as mine on this case. And so's my bootblack's! Why would a killer shoot through a newspaper? What's the idea? Unless you hit it the other day, when you said that a murder might be planned to look like a suicide. And who stood to gain in this case by a suicide?"

He stood turning the scrap of paper over in his

hand. There was no reasonable doubt that it was the one shown in the picture, or that it was a corner of the *Daily News;* and his own idea was that it had not been on the floor when the Squad had gone over the room, that scorched and torn as it was, it had not dropped until possibly the concussion of the flashlight for the pictures had loosened it.

"Would it be possible," I asked, "for someone to plan a murder so that it would look like an accident, or even suicide? But so that, in case he was suspected, he could produce this paper as a sort of alibi?"

"It would work, of course. But not if the paper is destroyed, young woman."

And then I told him of the strained relations of the past day or two between Mary and Hugo. He listened gravely.

"And then what?"

"It's clear, isn't it? Miss Juliet gave Mary that paper, and she destroyed it. Now Hugo finds you still on the case, and his alibi is gone."

He whistled, but the next minute he smiled. "And so it was Hugo who got out of the window? And Hugo for whom Paula Brent brought the ladder? It won't wash, Miss Pinkerton! It won't wash."

He went on to say that he had decided to release Paula Brent after I had gone that day; and that a check-up on Mr. Brent as to Monday night showed that he had been out of the city.

"So that's that. And now where are we?"

Then, without warning, a new element was introduced into the case.

124

CHAPTER XIII

The doorbell rang, and a little fussy man who gave his name as Henderson was at the door. He wanted to see the Inspector.

"I telephoned and learned that you were here," he said. "I'd like to see you alone." He eyed me.

"You can talk before this lady."

"Well, it's like this. I didn't pick up the paper until about an hour ago, and I saw that you had been questioning Paula Brent. I live near the Brents, Inspector, and I may know something. I don't know how important it is."

"Everything's important in this case," the Inspector said.

Mr. Henderson's story was brief and to the point. He lived behind the Brents, on the next street; that is, their back yards adjoined, or almost. There was an alley between, and so their garages were across from each other, with only about twenty-five feet, the width of the alley, between them. Next door to the Brent house was the residence of a man named Elliott, also with a garage.

On Monday night Mr. Henderson had taken his

family to the theater, arriving home at eleven o'clock. He had put his sedan away and gone to the house when his wife discovered that she had left her purse in the car. Somewhat annoyed, he had gone back to the garage, entering it by the narrow door toward the house.

At that moment Paula Brent drove her coupé into the Brent garage, and stopped the engine. Mr. Henderson was groping in the dark for his wife's bag, and she could have had no idea that he was there. But apparently someone had either been waiting for her in the garage or just outside of it, for the next moment he heard voices. One was hers; the other was that of Charlie Elliott, the son of the family in the next house. There was no doubt as to who it was, for she named him.

"Good heavens, Charlie Elliott! You scared me. What's the idea?"

"You know the idea, all right. Look here, Paula, haven't you made a fool of yourself long enough?"

"That's my business."

"And how about your people? What would they think if they knew what I do?"

"What *do* you know?"

Mr. Henderson was interested by that time, and rather thrilled, I gathered. But after that, their voices dropped. They were quarreling, he said, and he was sorry to hear it. Everybody in the neighborhood liked them both, and up to six months before they had been together most of the time.

"Looked like a real love affair," Mr. Henderson said. "I kind of liked to see it, myself. Good-looking young people, you know, and all that."

126

The quarrel was apparently a bitter one, for at last the Elliott boy had said that he was going to settle the matter once for all; see somebody and have it out with him.

"Not now!" Paula said.

"Right now!" was his reply, and he started down the alley. Mr. Henderson listened, and he was certain that Elliott did not go into his place at all, but went on down to the cross-street.

"But wait a minute," he said. "I've got ahead of my story. Before he left, he took something from her. I heard a sort of scuffle, and she said sharply, 'Give me that. Give me that, do you hear?'"

Mr. Henderson stopped to wipe his face with his handkerchief. "I came as a matter of duty, you understand," he said, in a different tone. "I like them both, and I don't believe that Charlie Elliott would kill anything. But I talked it over with my wife that night, and when she saw the paper this evening, she insisted that I see you."

"What time was it when young Elliott started?"

"About eleven fifteen, I imagine. And she didn't leave for ten minutes or so afterward."

"Oh! She left again?"

"Yes. She stayed there in the garage for some time. I gathered that she was crying and was pretty well upset, and I waited because—well, I was interested, and I didn't much like her being there alone and in trouble. As a matter of fact, I was seriously considering going over to see what I could do, when she started her car and went out again."

"What time was that?"

"It may have been eleven thirty, or thereabouts.

Long enough, anyhow, for my wife gave me the devil when I got back. She's rather nervous," he added sheepishly.

I could believe that. He offered a complete picture of the subdued and dominated husband as he stood in the Mitchell hall that night, giving evidence that he would infinitely have preferred keeping to himself.

He had little more to add. He had not heard Paula's car come back, but his wife said that she had got in shortly after three thirty. They had a clock which chimed the hours. He hated the thing, but his wife liked it. She didn't sleep very well, and it was company for her.

Mr. Henderson left shortly before Hugo and the deputy inspector returned, and I had little or no time to discuss the new turn events had taken before I was compelled to retreat to the sickroom. I noticed that the Inspector looked unusually grave, however.

He sent the deputy inspector away about a quarter to eleven, and then, with Hugo leading the way, he proceeded to make a minute inspection of the house from the basement to the upper floor. I saw him stop on the landing and inspect the locked and bolted door to the servants' quarters, and he even stooped and glanced at the clothing still lying on the stairs. He saw the inverted pocket, I imagine, for he straightened and glanced at Hugo. But Hugo was imperturbable.

It was midnight when he went away. Miss Juliet had wakened by that time, so I went down at half past twelve and heated a glass of milk for her. But I must admit I was not comfortable down there. A wind was blowing outside, and the kitchen wing seemed to be even more out of repair than the rest of the house. It creaked and groaned, and once I would have sworn that the tea-kettle moved right across the top of the stove! If it had been possible to gallop upstairs with a glass of hot milk in my hand, I would have done it! As it was, I went up with my head turned over my shoulder, until I got almost to the top of the stairs. Then I fixed my eyes on the landing, and if Miss Juliet had appeared there at that minute in her white nightgown, I dare say I would have died of heart failure.

But I got to the room safely enough, and after the old lady drank the milk, she grew drowsy. Just before she dozed off, however, she asked me if Hugo had gone to bed, and seemed disappointed to learn that he had.

"I want to see him," she said. "I must see him before Arthur comes back, in the morning. He has a right to know."

She did not explain that, so at one o'clock I put on my kimono and fixed my couch for the night.

Something roused me after I had been asleep an hour or so. It sounded like a door banging somewhere, and I looked at the luminous dial of my watch. It was two o'clock, and there was a real gale going outside, although the room was quiet enough. But as I lay there, a sudden gust came in over the transom, and I could dimly see, by the distant street lights, that the curtain at the window was blowing out, and flapping in the wind.

Out, and not in! That took a moment to register in my mind, and then it meant only one thing. Someone somewhere in the house had opened either an outside door or a window.

I sat up and stared over the foot of the bed at the door into the hall, and I admit that if the handle had so much as turned, I was prepared to let out a shriek that would have reached to the police station. But it did not, and I was drawing a real breath when something happened which set my heart to hammering again. Something fell in the hall, or rather on the stairs to the third floor. There was no crash, but a dull thud, and then a complete and utter silence. I knew at once what it was.

Somebody had been going up those stairs to the third floor, and had stumbled over the clothes piled on them.

CHAPTER XIV

For just a moment I had an irresistible impulse to crawl into bed beside Miss Juliet and cover my head with the bedclothes. The next, however, I was in the center of the floor, and listening intently. There was no further sound, and I moved to the door and put my ear against it.

There was no room for doubt. Someone was stealthily climbing the stairs to the third floor. The old stairs creaked one after the other, and one of the boards on the landing gave with a loud crack.

The next second I was out in the dark hall and feeling my way to the locked door to the back flat. I wanted Hugo; I wanted Hugo and Mary. I wanted somebody near, and the fact that, in spite of everything, I still suspected Hugo of the murder seemed at that minute to have no importance whatever.

In a condition approaching panic I groped my way through that awful darkness, and flung myself against the door. "Hugo!" I called. "Hugo!"

The next second I was falling, and that is all I remember.

When I came to, I was lying flat on my back in a

room I had never seen before, and Mary, in her nightgown, was sprinkling water on my face and listening to a crashing noise overhead which sounded like the breaking down of a door. Hugo was not in sight.

"Where am I?" I asked feebly.

"In our sitting room, miss," Mary said shortly. "You fainted."

I managed to sit up and look about me. From somewhere out in the grounds a man was calling, and from overhead came that continued battering, as though a heavy body was throwing itself against a door. Mary had left me and was standing in the doorway, listening; in the doorway, for that long-locked door onto the landing was standing wide open. But a strangely changed Mary. If ever I have seen a woman look tortured, she did that night. When I spoke again to her, she did not reply.

"It's a strong door," she said, as though she was talking to herself. "It looks old and easy to break, but it's strong."

"Who's in the room?" I demanded. "Is it Hugo?"

That seemed to register. She turned and gave me a strange look. "Hugo!" she said. "Hugo is up there helping the police."

And as if to prove it, there was a call above for an axe, and Hugo passed the open doorway on a run, going downstairs apparently to get one.

I got up then, rather dizzily, and surveyed the site of my recent disaster. The door from the little sitting room onto the landing was open, as I have said, and I could see readily enough what had happened. I had thrown myself against it, and it had been partly open.

In my fall I must have struck my head, perhaps on the rocker of a chair nearby, for I found a sharp bruise on my forehead later on.

The room itself was small and dreary enough, although it was very tidy. In a corner a small staircase led down into darkness, and I knew that it ended at the side door behind the parlor window. All this I took in at a glance: the room, the staircase, the open door and Mary in it. I moved unsteadily toward the doorway, to find her planted squarely in it.

"Better sit down and wait a minute, miss. You've had a bad knock."

"Let me out, Mary. I'm going upstairs."

She eyed me. "Nobody's going up those stairs," she said doggedly. "Let them fight it out themselves. You stay here."

"Don't be idiotic, Mary. I can at least go to see Miss Juliet."

She moved aside, unwillingly. "I wouldn't wonder there'll be shooting," she said. "He'll be desperate."

"He? Who?"

She shrugged her shoulders, under her cheap cotton nightgown. "You'll find out soon enough now," was all she would say, and again fell into that somber attitude of waiting and listening. For what? Even now I am uncertain as to how much Mary knew that night, or how much she merely suspected.

I looked in at Miss Juliet. She was wide awake, and staring at the door as I entered.

"What is it?" she asked anxiously. "Who is running up and down the stairs?"

Well, there was no use mincing matters. I shouted to her that the police were in the house, and that they had apparently trapped a burglar on the third floor; that he had locked himself in one of the rooms, and they were breaking down the door. But if I had expected her to show excitement, she did not.

"I hope they won't break the door," she said. "My father was so proud of the doors in this house. They are all solid walnut. Ask them to do as little damage as they can."

And that was that! I gazed at her in astonishment, but she only waved me toward the hall.

"Tell them, please."

I went out obediently, and over those piles of clothing to the upper hall. It was all a part of the strangeness of that night that I should find the Inspector there outside the closed door into Herbert's room, with Evans, the deputy inspector from Headquarters, and a lieutenant in uniform, and that none of them paid any attention to me. I can still see them, the Inspector with his gun in his hand, and the lieutenant now working with the axe. But as I arrived, the Inspector stopped them.

"Pretty solid door," he said. Then, raising his voice, he called, "Stand aside in there. I'm going to shoot this lock."

He waited a few seconds and then fired. The explosion fairly rocked the old house, but the door swung open, and the three men burst into the room. I was just behind them, and I saw standing against the wall by the head of the bed a tall, very good-looking young man, ghastly white, but with a faint smile on his face.

He moved away from the wall and faced us all

squarely, still with that faint whimsical smile. "Pretty good door!" he said. "Don't make them like that any more."

"Good, but not good enough," said the Inspector, fumbling in his pockets. "Look him over, Evans."

"I'm not armed."

"I'm not looking for a gun. I want a bunch of keys."

He shrugged at that, and submitted quietly while the deputy searched him, laying out on the bureau in methodical order what he found: a monogrammed handkerchief, a gold cigarette case, a wallet, some loose money, and last of all a key ring with a number of keys. The Inspector took these last, and the young man smiled again.

"Sorry, Inspector," he said. "I can identify them all; office key, keys to my car, keys to my home. That's all. You can try them out if you like."

"I wouldn't be feeling funny, if I were in your place," said the Inspector grimly. "Take these down and try them, Jim." He passed the keys to the lieutenant, who disappeared. "How did you get into this house?"

"Maybe I found the doors open."

But the Inspector merely grunted, and went to the window.

"O'Reilly," he called, "did this bird throw anything out of the window?"

"Didn't hear anything, Inspector."

"Well, take a look around. I want a bunch of keys."

He turned back to the boy. "I'm arresting you, Elliott. I guess you know why."

135

"Housebreaking?"

"That will do until we find those keys."

"And then what?"

"Then I'll arrest you for the murder of Herbert Wynne, in this room, last Monday night."

He fumbled in his pockets and brought out a pair of handcuffs, and for a second or so I thought the boy was going to faint. Then he straightened himself and smiled again, faintly.

"So I killed him," he said quietly. "I killed him, but I couldn't stay away from the scene of my crime! Like a dog returning to his vomit, eh?"

"I've told you it isn't funny."

"I'm not trying to be funny. I'm trying not to cry, or fight. You don't need the bracelets. I'm coming all right."

"You bet you're coming."

We stood there, waiting. The lieutenant brought back young Elliott's keys, reporting that none of them fitted the doors in question. In the grounds, O'Reilly and Evans, the deputy inspector, were searching below the window, presumably with a flashlight. In the doorway Hugo stood like a man carved out of stone, and down in Miss Juliet's room I could hear Mary shouting to her that they had caught the burglar.

Suddenly the boy lost his debonair manner. He looked at the Inspector with rather desperate young eyes. "I'd like to stop and tell my mother," he said. "She'd take it better from me. She hasn't been well, and this will be a shock to her."

"It's a little late to be thinking about a shock for

136

her, isn't it?" the Inspector said coldly.

The boy—he was not much more—made an odd little gesture, throwing out both hands in a helpless fashion that went to my heart. Then he got hold of himself again, shrugged his shoulders and put his hands in his pockets.

"Sorry!" he said. "My fault! Forgive these tears! And may I have a cigarette? No poison in them, save the natural poison of the natural leaf."

When no one spoke, he went to the bureau and took one from his case. In that brilliant light, with all eyes on him, he looked like a bright-haired young actor, rehearsing a bit of business. When he had lighted his cigarette, he flicked his eyes over us, and they came to rest on me. He stood looking at me thoughtfully.

"You, there," he said. "I don't know your name. Will you telephone a message for me?"

"To your mother?"

"I'll attend to that. To Paula Brent. You know her. In fact, I think you owe her something, don't you? If it hadn't been for you—but never mind that. Tell her there has been a slip-up, but she is not to worry. Will you?"

I glanced at the Inspector. But at that instant we heard the tramp of feet below, and soon after, Evans and O'Reilly came into the room. Evans held out his hand, without speaking. On his palm lay two keys on a silver ring, and he confronted the Elliott boy with them.

"These what you threw away?"

"That would be telling. Think it out for yourself,"

137

he said, with that white-lipped flippancy which fooled nobody.

"These are Herbert Wynne's keys, to the side door and to the door on the second-floor landing. His initials are on the key ring. How did you get them?"

"That," said young Elliott quietly, "I regard strictly as my own business."

CHAPTER XV

It was about half past two when they took him away. He walked down the stairs jauntily enough, and he went down without the bracelets after all. I think the Inspector felt a sort of grudging admiration for the way he had carried it off, and after all there were four of them to guard him. I stood in the hall and watched that heavy footed procession go out the front door, and something in me rebelled. That boy a killer!

Yet I knew that the case against him was practically complete, so far as the police were concerned. He had a motive, as Mr. Henderson and a good many other people knew; he had been in love with Paula Brent, probably still was. He had left her in anger on Monday night, to go and settle the matter with someone unknown. She had been frightened and had followed him somewhat later; and that the somebody he meant to settle with was Herbert Wynne was certain, for it was to the Mitchell house that she had gone.

It was one of those neatly fitting cases that the

Inspector loved, as I knew. Every piece fell into place, now that he had the keys. Here was the Elliott boy in Herbert's room that night, and old Miss Juliet unconsciously cutting off his retreat; and here was the open window, and his strong young arms to swing him to the roof below, and safety. But not immediate safety. There must have been a bad time when the Inspector threw his flashlight out onto that roof; the boy cowering behind the chimney, and the flash playing on both sides of him.

Just how Paula had discovered him there I did not know. It seemed certain, however, that she had, that she had then gone in search of a ladder, dragged it to the house and so enabled him to escape. And I had not the slightest doubt that it was Charles Elliott who, as the man in the dinner jacket, had returned the ladder to the Manchester property.

Tragic as the situation was, I had to smile at the sheer audacity with which that entire escape was carried through, and at the thought of Inspector Patton smoking quietly on the front porch, while those two youngsters calmly used that ladder and then politely returned it to where it belonged. As a matter of fact, later on we were to learn that when the Inspector left me Monday night to investigate a sound at the rear of the house, he almost fell over that ladder as it lay on the ground.

That was one time when his theory of working in the dark failed him!

But I only learned that later, and after much grief and further trouble had made all that relatively unimportant. What I knew that night, as they took the boy away, was that he was in line for the chair;

140

and I felt I could not bear it.

I knew well enough what would happen. I had seen it too often. The District Attorney's office would make its case, using only what it required to do so, and eliminating everything which conflicted with it. That scrap of powder-stained newspaper would never be brought into evidence; nor another thing which occurred to me as I once more prepared for what was left of the night. Herbert had started to undress when he was shot. That didn't look as though Charlie Elliott had entered the house with him; and if he had not, then how had he got in?

It was easy enough to explain his presence this night, provided he had killed Herbert. He could have taken the keys from his pocket. They were Herbert's own keys. But on Monday night he would not have had those keys. And again, even granting that he had killed Herbert Wynne, why had he taken the keys from him? What mystery lay behind them, and his reckless entrance tonight into the house which, above all others, he should have avoided? And was this his first visit? What about that figure I had seen on the landing, the night I had found Hugo asleep in the parlor? What about the man who had bumped into Florence Lenz? Had Charlie Elliott been that figure, that man?

I sat down on my sofa and held my head. I had a lump the size of a goose egg on it, and my brain felt like a cheese soufflé, but I had to do my thinking then, if ever; I knew that something terrible was going to happen if I did not.

Miss Juliet was awake but quiet, and in the lower hall I could hear Hugo at the telephone, reporting

141

the night's events to Doctor Stewart and to Mr. Glenn. Mary was nowhere in sight; I had seen her face as Charlie Elliott was taken downstairs, and it had puzzled me even in that moment of stress. She had looked at the boy, and then she had turned hard relentless eyes on Hugo, following the others. But he had not looked at her.

It was the door on the landing, I found, which most puzzled me. That is, outside of Charlie Elliott being in the house that night at all. I gave that up. It seemed plain idiocy to me, for if he had left anything incriminating there, he must have known that the Homicide Squad would have found it, unless it was that he was afraid he had left some prints on the window sill.

That was possible, and after Hugo had hung up the receiver below and gone to bed, I invented an excuse and went up to look. But if Charlie Elliott had left any readable prints on that sill—and I had the Inspector's word that he had not—there was no sign of them now. Only in one corner a bit of the print powder which the police had used on them.

I stood there, looking around that bare little room. Like the rest of the house, Herbert Wynne might never have lived there, for any trace of occupancy he had left. But I noticed something that the police had apparently overlooked. The bed had been moved somewhat. It stood four or five inches away from the wall, and not entirely straight.

It must have been three o'clock by that time, and three o'clock in the morning is a low hour for nurses as well as patients. But I had to look under that bed, and around it. I hated the room; I hated the whole job. Nevertheless I examined it carefully, and, finding nothing, I got down on the floor and crawled under it. I had had one case where an important paper was hidden under a bed slat, and I was not going to make another mistake.

But as I have said, that room was filled with ghosts for me, and my head was jumping anyhow. I got underneath somehow, and on my back at that; and I had no sooner done so than something touched my ankle. I lay there, helpless and absolutely paralyzed, and the next minute it gave another soft shove against my knee.

Then I yelped, and I imagine I hold the world's record for the lying broad leap. I simply gathered my muscles together and shot out, and why I didn't carry the bed with me I do not know. I was out in the hall before I dared to look back. Then I saw that it was Mary's cat again; and if I had bitten it that night, it would have died of tetanus.

I suppose, in order to make it interesting at this point, I should have gone back into the room and found a clue there. But it has not been my experience that criminals go about dropping cuff-links for the police to discover. And I did not go back into that room. Not that night, at least.

A nurse has to learn to act, and so I probably looked calm enough when I went back to Miss Juliet. She was still awake. Although she had accepted the story of a burglar calmly, I was not sure that she had believed it, and I have wondered since if some inkling of the truth had come to her that night. Did she know she was in danger? How could she know?

I cannot think so, and yet something she requested

might be so construed. I had been rubbing her with alcohol, after that experience on the third floor, when unexpectedly she said, "I shall want to see my clergyman tomorrow, Miss Adams."

"Very well, Miss Juliet."

"I want to make a statement to my lawyer first, and then to speak to my clergyman. Mary knows who he is. You can tell her."

"A statement? Can't that wait until you are stronger?"

"I may never be any stronger," she said, in her flat voice. And added, as if to reassure me, "After all, I am an old woman, my dear. I am living on borrowed time at the best."

I did the usual thing, of course; told her she was getting better all the time, and so on. But my mind was occupied with only the one thing. She was going to make a statement of some sort! A formal statement, signed.

I took that to my sofa with me later, along with my bump and my headache. What sort of statement? Would it involve Charlie Elliott still further? After all, what had she seen that night when she climbed the stairs? What had she told Mr. Glenn so that he would say, or shout, "I don't believe it. I don't care what he told you. I don't believe it."

I had thought that that had referred to Herbert, but did it? Suppose that when Miss Juliet went up the stairs Monday night, she had found Charlie Elliott in the room above? Suppose, then, that all the time she lay in her bed, and I on the couch at its foot, she had known that he was on the roof? And suppose that her later excursion to the third floor while I slept was to see if he was still there, or had escaped?

Then all those days she had lain in her bed, knowing something which she had concealed. And now she was about to tell it, and to send that boy to the chair. To save her own soul, and send him to the chair! Her lawyer and then her clergyman, and that bright-haired boy her burnt offering.

It made me shudder.

I was convinced that I was right, but it was daylight before I thought of a plan, and that not a very hopeful one. Yet, in a way, it had possibilities. After all, it was her indignation that Paula Brent had been questioned by the police which had apparently crystallized her resolution. Evidently that ancient love affair of hers with Paula's grandfather had never been entirely forgotten. And my plan was simply to get Paula there before the attorney came, and to have her plead with the old lady for silence.

I think now that it would have worked, and I put it among the tragic failures of my career that I did not make myself clear when I finally got Paula on the telephone. She understood well enough. She agreed to come. But what with her terror and excitement over the news of Charlie Elliott's arrest, she somehow mistook the hour. I had told her nine o'clock, and she came at ten.

She was just an hour too late.

CHAPTER XVI

I hope never to live through another morning like that one of Friday, the eighteenth of last September.

The first thing that went wrong was the arrival of Inspector Patton, slightly smug with success and, what is rare with him, inclined to be garrulous. That was at half past eight, and Paula was due at nine. He had apparently settled the case and thrown all caution to the winds, for he called me down into the library and closed the door.

"You look half dead," he observed, inspecting me. "You'll need a rest after this case. But I guess it's over."

"Naturally!" I said with some bitterness. "I know it. Who better? Why should you care whether he did it or not? You've got your case, and that's what you want, isn't it?"

"You're like all women. Because a man happens to be good-looking, you can't believe he's a rascal."

"I can't believe he's a fool, either. Why did he come back again, last night? And maybe a night or so ago, too? Tell me that."

"What does it matter, now? We're not interested in

last night, or the night before. We're interested in Monday night, and that's all."

"You would be!" I said. "Personally, I don't think you've touched this story. You've got your case, but you have enough left over to make another. Why did Charlie Elliott fire that shot through a newspaper?"

He smiled. "Who said he did? That scrap of paper was from a *News* of the week before."

I stared at him. "A week old?"

"Our fellows looked it up. No mistake about it, Miss Pinkerton! And as for his coming back, you know why he did that, and so do I."

"I suppose you mean the prints on the window sill?"

"I thought you'd get that. Yes."

He settled down in his chair and drew out his pipe, and I had a cold sensation of despair. He was going to go over the whole story. I knew what that meant. So long as he remained around the place, I could not smuggle Paula into Miss Juliet's room. And it was no use to try to escape. When I said my patient needed me, he merely called to Hugo to tell Mary to stay with her, and calmly went on talking.

Under any other circumstances I would have been interested, to say the least; and even as it was, I followed him clearly enough, if I did spend most of the time watching the drive for Paula Brent. He explained first what, to me at least, had remained a mystery so far, just how and why he had had the house surrounded, and had caught Charlie Elliott as he had. After that semi-absurd watch of the night before, divided between Mr. Glenn and the doctor, he had put a man on the grounds "on general principles," as he said. But also, after hearing Mr. Henderson's story the evening before, he had had young Elliott "tailed." He had put a good operative on the case, and then had gone back to his office.

"You see, I held something out on you that I'd known for a day or two," he said, eying me. "No use making you nervous, you know. That bolt on the door upstairs, the one on the landing, wasn't much use. Not any, in fact. It had been sawed off, so that it appeared to be on the job, but wasn't. It fooled me for a while. It fitted pretty closely, and there was no key to unlock the door and test it. It stood to reason, then, that anybody with keys to that door and to the side door below could get in and out whenever they wanted. That's what Herbert Wynne did, anyhow. In spite of the old lady, he could come and go at night pretty much as he liked, provided, of course, the servants had gone to bed."

"Did Hugo know about the bolt?"

"He says he didn't."

"And you believe that?"

"I believe this. I believe Hugo was as worried about this fellow getting into the house as anybody, and as puzzled."

But that door, and its sawed-off bolt, had played their part in what he called the solution of the crime.

"Elliott had to get in somehow," he said. "He got in Monday night and committed the murder. He got part of the way in on Tuesday night, and you spoiled it. He escaped through the door on the landing, of course; again on Wednesday night, when he knocked down Glenn's secretary and gave her a sore knee for him to be sorry for." He grinned. "And again

149

last night.

"Now it isn't hard to know how he got in. He'd taken those keys from the body, so that was simple enough. But how did he get in the first night? That's the question."

"He won't tell you?"

"No."

"You surprise me!" I said, with the sarcasm he detests.

"Still fighting for the blond-haired boy!" he observed. "Well, that comes of letting a woman in on a thing like this. She gets carried away by her emotions."

"*Letting* me in? I was dragged in, and you know it."

He let that go, and went back to the story of the night before. After Mr. Henderson's statement, he had put the operative on the case, and then gone to his office at Headquarters. He often sleeps there, and he had had a hunch that something might happen.

It did. At half past one the operative watching the Elliott house had seen young Elliott slip out quietly, using a rear door and not taking his car, and having followed him to the Mitchell property, found the policeman hidden in the shrubbery on the other side of the house and notified him. Then he had hurried to the nearest telephone and called Headquarters.

When the Inspector and Evans arrived, young Elliott had already entered the house by the side entrance, and they found the door there standing open. They had brought a police lieutenant along also, and he remained outside at first, to watch with O'Reilly for a possible escape.

150

The Inspector and Evans had gone in by the same route, moving very quietly, and they had just reached the top of the stairs when they had what amounted to a real shock, there in the servants' sitting room and in black darkness. Something had given a terrible shriek and then pitched into the room almost at their feet, and not moved.

"That was you," said the Inspector, "and the only reason I didn't turn and bolt down those stairs was because Evans was behind me!"

Well, they turned a flash on me, and at first they thought I had been killed.

"It was a bad thirty seconds or so," the Inspector said, smiling grimly. "It looked as though he'd got you. I don't mind telling you that I thought I'd lost my most valuable assistant!"

But the beans were spilled by that time, he said. There had been enough noise to rouse everybody in the house, and to warn Elliott.

"He was warned all right. A dynamite explosion couldn't have done it any better! But he couldn't get out this time. He might have tried the roof again, but had no little lady friend to help him down, and he probably saw our fellows below anyhow. What he did was to lock the door and then wait. He hadn't anything to gain by it, but that's what he did. Just to make it harder!"

"Or to gain time to look for whatever he was after," I said. "I suppose that hadn't occurred to you?"

"The prints on the sill? He'd had plenty of time for that."

"But he didn't touch them, did he?"

He looked at me thoughtfully. "Well, no. Now

151

that you speak of it, he didn't. But he didn't have to. As he swung off, he'd smeared them pretty well, and he'd realized that. What are you driving at?"

"I'm intimating that he was there to get something," I said rather sharply. "And that it was not fingerprints, unless they were under the bed."

"Under the bed? Nonsense!"

"Then why was the bed moved away from the wall? Or perhaps you didn't notice that?"

He got up, and grinned rather sheepishly. "One up for you," he said. "No, I didn't notice it. I'm a rotten policeman, but you're the only one who knows it! I'll go up and take a look around!"

But he did not go at once. "What are you thinking about this case?" he asked. "You've got an opinion. I can see that. And it's not mine."

"It is not. There was a time when you were certain this case was a suicide, and I believed it was a murder. Perhaps you remember that? Now you would stake your reputation that it was a murder, and . . ."

"And that I have the murderer. I certainly would. Well?"

"I'm still trying to explain to myself why that scrap of newspaper had powder marks on it. And whether, after all, Paula Brent doesn't believe that Herbert left a letter explaining that he had killed himself, and sent that boy to get it. How deep was he in the market?"

"All he had. That wasn't enough to drive him to suicide."

"Well then, something which might explain this danger he was always talking about."

"How do you know there was such a danger? Or

that the girl didn't invent that story later on, to protect this Elliott boy?"

"He was carrying a gun. Monday night wasn't the first night Herbert had carried that gun."

"How do you know he was, before that night? That's her story, too."

"All right," I said. "Then tell me where he got the money to take out all that insurance? And enough more to speculate with on a margin? That's what you've got left over, isn't it? You've got your case, but you have all that left over. What are you going to do about it?"

He did not answer that, for the telephone rang, and as it was the District Attorney, he had to leave at once and go downtown.

When I saw him again, it was too late. The second tragedy had happened.

CHAPTER XVII

When he had gone, I took a final despairing look outside, but Paula was still not in sight, and so I went up to Miss Juliet. To my surprise Mary was not there, and it was Hugo who stood by the bed. It was the first time I had seen him in the room, and if ever I have seen a man both alarmed and angry, he was that morning. He was standing by the bed, and Miss Juliet was talking, in her low monotonous voice. The door was open, and when he heard me on the landing, he made a gesture of caution and her voice ceased.

He brushed past me without a word, and soon after that Mr. Glenn arrived, and I heard Hugo talking to him in the lower hall. He was still upset, apparently, and Mr. Glenn seemed to be conciliating him. However that was, Hugo came up in a few minutes to say that the lawyer wanted to see me in the library, and so I went down again.

Rather to my surprise, I found the secretary in the hall. She was standing in front of the mirror powdering her nose, and she grinned at me in the glass.

155

"You don't feel weak, or anything?" she sang out at me.

"Weak? Why?"

"I'd like to try that ammonia stunt on you, for a change!"

"The next time you throw a fit like that, be sure there's no trained nurse around," I told her, and went into the library.

Mr. Glenn was there, neat and immaculate and rather too well dressed, as usual. But he was nervous, too. He was pacing up and down the room when I entered it.

"This is a bad business, Miss Adams," he said. "Very bad indeed."

"Does Miss Juliet know about it?"

"Not yet. No."

"That's right. Keep it from her as long as you can. Tell Mary not to carry her a paper. I can trust Hugo, but not Mary." He took another turn about the room, while I stood waiting. "As a matter of fact, I think the old lady knows already that this boy is guilty, Miss Adams. She intimated as much to me last night."

"Then why keep the arrest from her?" I asked. "After all, if she knows . . ."

He hesitated. "I suppose I might as well tell you. She intends to make a statement this morning. Or perhaps you know that."

"I do."

"Well, this statement should be as unprejudiced as possible. She saw something last Monday night, and that is what she wants to tell."

"She saw Charlie Elliott, I suppose, Mr. Glenn?"

"That's for her to say," he said shortly. "The point

156

is that, right or wrong, she thinks she has not long to live, and she wants to tell her story before she goes. As a matter of fact, it was to be kept in my safe, and only used in case of some miscarriage of justice. But this arrest changes things. She needn't know that, however."

"She needn't make the statement at all!" I said. And then, what with Paula not getting there in time and strain and lack of sleep and all the rest, I simply made a fool of myself and burst into tears.

I could hear him talking, but I could not stop crying. He said the police had the case anyhow, and that everybody knew that Charlie Elliott had been crazy about Paula for years; and jealous of her, too. But when he went upstairs, I was still crying, and that gibbering idiot of a Florence was standing in the doorway staring at me with hard amused eyes.

"And did she get her feelings hurt!" she said. "And didn't he pet her, or anything?"

"Oh, for God's sake keep quiet," I said, and went out on the porch for air and to escape from her. I found Paula just coming up the steps.

She was white and distracted, and I had to draw her around the corner of the house, for Florence was watching from the hall. I was ready to shout at her, to tell her what the delay had cost; but one look at her was enough, and anyhow it was too late. She looked as nearly frantic as I have ever seen a human being look, and she simply caught at me and held on.

"Is the Inspector here?" she demanded. "I've got something to tell him. Are they all crazy, down there?"

"They found him, here in the house."

157

"Is the Inspector here? Don't talk. Tell me!"

"The District Attorney sent for him. Now listen, Paula. Try to be quiet and listen to me. There's no hurry. You've got months; weeks, anyhow. What you have to tell the Inspector can wait."

"But it can't wait. Why should Charlie Elliott be under arrest, when I ought to be?"

I almost shook her. "Don't talk like that. You didn't kill Herbert Wynne, and you know it."

"I got Charlie into this mess," she said doggedly. "I've got to get him out. Listen, Miss Adams, I gave him those keys he had last night. They were mine."

"*You* gave them to him?"

"Don't look at me like that. I don't care what you think about me. I gave him those keys, to get something of mine that I'd left in that room."

It is not easy to shock me, but I was shocked at that moment. By and large, I know as much as anyone about the free and easy ways of this generation of youngsters, and I have always believed that the free and easiness is a matter of manners, not morals. It seems strange now, but my first reaction had nothing to do with murder, but with the fact that this girl, wide-eyed and young, had had keys which had enabled her to visit Herbert Wynne in that upper room of his; and that she had done so.

But I rallied myself, and I hope my face showed nothing. Not that I think she would have noticed, anyhow.

"What was it that you had left in that room?"

"My bag."

"And when?"

She hesitated, and looked at me with quick

suspicion. "I'd rather talk to the Inspector."

"And make things worse!" I said. "I'm friendly, at least. I warn you now that the Inspector is not. Nor any of the police. When did you give Charlie Elliott those keys?"

"I don't see——"

"Listen," I said brutally. "Do you want to send him to the chair? Don't you see what I mean? If you go to the police and tell them that Charlie Elliott had your keys on last Monday night, that's the end of him."

She paled, and drew a quick breath.

"I'll tell you this, for your own sake," I went on. "They know a lot that you don't realize; they know about the ladder, and they think they know who got it, for one thing. Maybe they can't prove that, but they'll try. And they know that Charlie Elliott was jealous of Herbert, and that you two quarreled about him on Monday night. What's the use of making things worse by telling about those keys until you have to? And damaging your reputation into the bargain?"

She lifted her chin at that. "I've done nothing I'm ashamed of," she said. "And I've told you part of the truth anyhow. Charlie Elliott came here last night on an errand for me."

"To get your bag? Don't be foolish."

"To get something."

I turned as if to go. "All right," I said. "I've done my best for you. Maybe you'd better run to Police Headquarters and let them work on you for a little while. I have a lot of things to do."

But she ran after me and caught my arm. "Listen,"

159

she said. "I've got to talk to somebody, and I know you're friendly. It wasn't a bag. It was a letter. I've told you there was a letter."

"You'll have to go further than that," I said shortly. "If you know something that will help Charlie Elliott out of this trouble, I'm simply telling you that I'd be glad to hear about it, and to help if I can. If that isn't enough, then I'll go back to my patient. What about this letter, and where is it? You'd better come clean."

"I'll tell you," she said in an exhausted voice. "Can't we sit down somewhere? I haven't slept or eaten for days."

She looked it, too, poor child. I found an old bench in a corner of the grounds, somewhat screened from the house, and there she tried to tell me what she knew. It was not a great deal, as it turned out, and it sounded rather fantastic, to tell the truth, when I finally did get it.

Some of it, of course, I already knew. Within the last few months, Herbert had got mixed up in something shady. She thought that it involved Hugo, but whatever it was—and obviously she did not know except that it was "not bootlegging"—it had finally dawned on him that Hugo, or whoever it was, was not playing fair with him; and that he was possibly in danger of his life.

It was after they were fired at that he began to talk of their going away together. She knew then that he was frightened, and she tried to get from him what the trouble was, and who was after him. But he would not tell her. But here came the matter of the letter again.

"I'll put that in a letter and leave it for you," he told her. "So if somebody gets me, you can pin the rap on the proper party!"

He had said it with a laugh, but the idea had taken hold of her, and she insisted that he do it.

"You can see why," she told me. "It wasn't that I wanted it for that reason; but if he wrote such a letter, and Hugo, or whoever it was, knew there was such a letter, it would keep him from—bothering Herbert."

Well, it was not a bad idea at that, and it appeared that Herbert had thought so, too, after a long delay. There had been no more trouble, apparently, after that one attempt to shoot him; and on that last night, Monday, he had been very cheerful.

"I've got it all set down, honey," he told her. "But I think it's all right anyhow. We'll be getting out of here pretty soon. As soon as the market settles down."

He had promised to give her the letter the next day, and she was to place it in a bank vault. In the meantime he had hidden it in a safe place; she thought in his own room.

I have said that it sounded fantastic; like the juvenile vaporings of an immature mind, trying to impress a romantic girl by working on her fears and her sense of drama. But there is something fantastic about all unusual crimes, and after all, there was that shot to account for. Also I remembered something the Inspector had said to me when I took my first case for him. "Working on crime is a lot like working in a steel mill; never sit down on anything until you spit on it first. It may be hot."

But the point of all this was that, after Monday night, first Paula herself, and later Charlie Elliott, had set to work to find that letter, and had failed. I tried to think that out.

"Then," I said, "it was this letter that Charlie Elliott was trying to find last night?"

"Yes. I'd tried to once myself, but you came up the stairs. You may remember. You screamed."

Did I remember! I would have shaken her then and there, small and woebegone as she looked.

"And nothing else? Just a letter?"

I thought she was less assured when she replied to that. "What else could there be?"

"And it hasn't been found?"

She shook her head. "I don't think it is there," she said. "I think they got it and destroyed it."

And by "they" once more I knew she meant the people in the house.

CHAPTER XVIII

Standing there with the wind blowing my uniform about me, I had a moment of doubt. Never before had I worked against the Inspector, and I felt disloyal and uncomfortable. Yet the Inspector wanted the facts, and if this girl offered one way to get at them, then it seemed to me that it was my duty to use her.

But I was convinced that Paula had not told me all the truth. Indeed, had it not been that the letter had not been found, I might have gone so far as to suspect her of planting such a letter after the crime! Certain as she was that someone inside that house had killed Herbert Wynne, she might conceivably have gone even to such a length to bring out what she felt were the facts.

But the letter had not been found, and inside that house I was certain that old Miss Juliet Mitchell was at that moment making her peace with her God, and was about to sign Charlie Elliott's death warrant.

I was roused by Paula touching my arm. "Listen," she said. "Why can't you get me into that house and upstairs? Now."

"I might, if you had come clean as I asked you."

163

She colored faintly. "I've told you all I can," she said. "I'll give you my word for this, Miss Adams. I'll show whatever I find to you. Absolutely. And you can tell the police."

"Then, you know where this letter is? Or was?"

"I think I do. I'm not certain."

"Why not let *me* look?"

But she made an impatient gesture. "Why should I?" she demanded. "I've trusted you, and I think you're friendly. But this is a life and death matter, and after all *they* employ you." She changed her tone. "I'm sorry, but you'll not regret it. I promise you that."

I agreed, at last. Agreed with an uncomfortable feeling that Paula was probably being shadowed all the time, and that the Inspector might come down on me with one of his rare rages when he found it out. She followed me to the front of the house, and rather to my surprise it was empty. Florence Lenz had disappeared and there was no sign of Hugo. The house was very quiet, except for Mary, scrubbing viciously somewhere in the rear.

I turned and nodded to Paula, and she slipped in, looking about her nervously. Everything was quiet as we reached the landing; Miss Juliet's door was still closed, and from behind it came the faint monotonous sound of her voice. But just as I reached the door leading into my own room, which adjoined Miss Juliet's, I heard Hugo's heavy step in the hall overhead. He was coming down from the third floor.

Both of us stopped, petrified. Then I caught Paula and shoved her—there is no other word—into my room and followed her. As I closed the door, Hugo was on the stairs above! I stood for a moment, facing the door and holding the knob, and I confess that my heart was beating a good hundred and fifty, and then some. Hugo did not stop, however. I thought he hesitated outside of Miss Juliet's door, but he went on again, and I waited until I could hear him in the lower hall before I turned.

Florence was in front of the dressing table, staring at Paula with her hard curious eyes. She had been powdering her nose, and using my powder to do it. The puff was still in her hand.

"Miss Brent, isn't it?"

"Never mind," I said shortly. "This young lady wants to talk to me. If you have anywhere else to go, I'd like my room for a few minutes."

But she was quite impervious to sarcasm. Indeed, I doubt if she heard me at all. There was a twisted little smile on her face by that time, and she ran her eyes over Paula, beginning at her feet and ending at her face.

"I'm Florence Lenz," she said. "Maybe you've heard of me?"

She meant something by that. I knew it, and Paula knew it. She drew herself up and gave the other girl look for look.

"Possibly. Is there any particular reason why I should?"

"There's plenty of reason, and you damned well know it," Florence retorted, reddening under her coating of powder. But she seemed to make an effort then, and pulled herself together.

"Mr. Glenn sent for me to come up," she explained to me. "Then the old woman in there thought of something else, so I wandered in here. I'm a notary, and she is to sign something." Her eyes flickered to

Paula again, standing stiff and straight, and then to me. "Making a will, isn't she? She's got plenty of money now."

That, too, I felt, was for Paula. The scene, if it could be called that, had no meaning for me; but it had meaning. I knew it, or felt it. And I felt that for some unknown reason Paula was slowly reaching a breaking point. She was entirely colorless by that time, and rigid.

I went to the hall door and opened it, but although Hugo had disappeared, Mary was in the hall now. Ostensibly she was moving that clothing which still lay, trampled from the night before, on the stairs. Actually she was close to the door of Miss Juliet's room, and although her arms were loaded, I was certain that she had been listening with her ear to the door.

She started and moved away when she saw me, and I waited until she had gone down the stairs. Halfway down, she looked up again, and I began to think that I was developing a complex about Mary; that I was always looking down at her from those stairs, and she looking up with wary eyes, watching me.

Maybe I only imagine all that. Maybe, as I look back over the case, I remember certain incidents and give them a value they did not have at the time. But Mary looked back right enough, and then stumbled over a dragging garment and almost fell. And back of me in that room Paula Brent certainly stood, icily still, while Florence made up her mouth and watched her in the mirror.

I gave Paula a quick look, and motioned to the hall. "We'll have to talk another time, Miss Brent," I told her. "If you don't mind waiting somewhere, I can see you later."

I closed the door behind her when she went, and I knew well enough that she was on her way to the third floor almost before I could turn around. I glanced at the dressing table, and sure enough there was powder all over it; over my instruments and my hypodermic tray as well, and I gave that young woman a piece of my mind as I straightened it. But I might as well have reproved one of the old silhouettes framed on the wall. She never even heard me.

"Is there any particular reason why I should know her?" she repeated. "I'll say there is. And I'll say she's got a hell of a lot of nerve, hanging around this house!"

Only the opening of the connecting door saved me from a charge of assault and battery with intent to kill. It was Mr. Glenn, and he seemed relieved to find me there.

"Come in, Miss Adams," he said, "and you, too, Miss Lenz. I want you to witness a signature."

He looked disturbed and very sober, and I saw that he had a paper in his hand. To my surprise I found Hugo there, also. Miss Juliet, her eyes closed, was lying back on the pillows; and I saw that Florence, well dusted with powder, was gazing at her with an expression of avid interest. From the bed her eyes traveled about the room, taking in every detail of its worn dignity, its shabby gentility.

Mr. Glenn had approached the bed. "You won't think better of this, Miss Juliet?" he said.

She sensed what he said rather than heard it, and shook her head. "I must do what is right, Arthur. I'm sorry; but I have told you the truth. Now let me

167

sign it."

He turned to us. Hugo had not moved.

"I have read this statement to Miss Mitchell. She acknowledges it to be correct, but while she wishes to sign it before witnesses, she prefers to keep the contents secret, for the time at least. Is that correct?" He looked at her.

"It is correct, Arthur."

So the four of us stood by while she signed with his pen, in a wavering old hand that still had some faint distinction: "Juliet Mitchell." Then she herself took it, folded it over so that only the signature showed, and Hugo and I both wrote our names in the opposite corner. Hugo's hand, I noticed, was shaking. That finished, Florence affixed her notarial seal and Mr. Glenn put the paper carefully into his brief case, and went back to the bed.

"I suppose you realize the importance of what you have done, Miss Juliet?" he said impressively. "What it means to several people."

She nodded. "I know you have tried, Arthur. But I have not long to live, and I must right a great injustice."

I thought she glanced at Hugo as she said that. But he said nothing. He turned and went out of the room, and Mr. Glenn followed him almost immediately, taking Florence with him.

I had plenty to think about for the next fifteen minutes or so; so much that I almost forgot Paula. For one thing, Miss Juliet's pulse was thin and reedy, and she seemed exhausted to the point of coma. It was not until I had telephoned for Doctor Stewart and had gone into my room for some spirits of ammonia that I really thought of Paula at all, and then it was

168

because I found her there, looking utterly dispirited.

"I can't get out," she said. "Hugo is sweeping the hall."

"Did you find anything?"

She shook her head hopelessly. "They've got it," she said. "And if that old woman in there knows it, then death is too good for her."

She did not mention Florence at all.

I went back to Miss Juliet. I had not told the girl about that scene which had just ended, and I did not intend to. It seemed to me that if that statement of the old lady's incriminated Charlie Elliott, Paula would learn it soon enough; and I had a shrewd idea, too, that in spite of everything she was more fond of Charlie Elliott than she realized. That Herbert's death had horrified rather than grieved her, and that her romance or infatuation, or whatever it might have been, had been almost over when he died.

I did not see Paula again until that evening. When Doctor Stewart came and I went in again for my hypodermic, she was gone.

All this which I have just written took place on Friday morning, the eighteenth of September. Herbert Wynne had been dead for almost four days, and Charlie Elliott had been under arrest since the night before. From the absence of reporters at the doorbell and in the grounds I gathered that public interest now centered around Police Headquarters; but shortly after Mr. Glenn left, somewhere around eleven o'clock, I saw two young men in paint-spattered overalls carrying a long ladder in through the gates, and I went to the back window of my room and watched them as they went around the house.

They were quite businesslike, but apparently they

had forgotten their paint! They put the ladder up against the wall not far from my window, and both climbed to the roof of the ell.

Well, my patience was pretty much exhausted by that time, so I got a broom from the housemaid's closet in the hall and, reaching out the window, I gave that ladder a good shove. It fell with a crash, and the last I saw of those two reporters they were peering dejectedly over the tin gutter of the roof, and muttering to themselves. Later on I learned that they had stayed on that roof for five hours, not daring to call for help! And it was a tin roof, and a hot September day.

I never thought of them again. It appears that one or two cameramen from other papers appeared, and that they appealed for help from them. But one rude young competitor only put his thumb to his nose at them, and another took their pictures. It was the police who rescued them at last, after threatening to leave them there all night.

Sometimes I think of them, marooned on that roof while, inside the house, a tragedy was taking place; probably seeing the Medical Examiner's car in the drive and people coming and going, going slowly crazy while another story broke, and nothing to do about it except, like Charlie Elliott, either to fight or cry.

But they served a very important purpose, nevertheless, in the answer to our mystery. When the dénouement came, it was as though we had been putting together one of those jigsaw puzzles, and they had found the key to the picture.

Mr. Glenn had not left the house until after eleven o'clock, and so it was probably nearly twelve when

170

the doctor arrived. I knew that it was after one when the Inspector, hurriedly sent for, was reached while he was eating his lunch, and he got there shortly afterward.

Just when Paula Brent left the house I do not know.

What happened, as accurately as I can remember, was as follows:

The doctor had ordered a hypodermic of nitroglycerin for Miss Juliet, and he remained with her, his fingers on her thin wrist, while I went down to the kitchen for some sterile water with which to give it. Mary was alone in the kitchen, and gave it to me herself.

I cleaned my hypodermic, and then, going back to my tray, I got the tube of tablets. There was no mistake about it. I remember looking at the label of the tube, which was not a fresh one, shaking out the tablet, dropping it into the glass barrel of the syringe, and watching it dissolve there. I remember all that, just as I remember pinching up the flesh of Miss Juliet's withered old arm, and her wincing at the jab of the needle. I remember, too, that Doctor Stewart still held his fingers on her pulse, and that I moved about the room, straightening it after my habit; and that I then went into the bathroom, where I washed my hypodermic needle and cleaned it with alcohol.

I was there when the doctor called to me. Miss Juliet looked rather strange. She had grown tense and was twitching somewhat. The doctor was leaning over her.

"What is it? Pain?"

She did not say anything, and he looked puzzled. "What did you give her?" he asked me.

171

"Just the usual dose of nitroglycerin, doctor."

That apparently satisfied him, and he drew up a chair and sat beside the bed. After ten minutes or so the twitching stopped, but she still seemed rather rigid, so he ordered another hypodermic. The interval between them was perhaps a half hour. I could feel that curious rigidity when I gave the second injection, but I had seen angina before, and some people stiffen under the pain.

I repeated my previous procedure, went to the bathroom, cleaned the syringe, put away my tray. I was in my room when I heard the doctor again, and this time he was fairly shouting for me.

I ran back, to see Miss Juliet in a convulsion on the bed.

Over and over again I have lived those next few minutes. I have even dreamed about them. In these dreams I am once again beside the big walnut bed, with Doctor Stewart across from me and staring down at the old lady, and she is having that convulsion, jerking and twitching; and on her unconscious face that dreadful *risus sardonicus*, the sardonic grin which almost at once began to fade into the mask of death.

How long that lasted I do not know. Time means nothing in such a situation. As the grin began to fade, I remember that I glanced up at the doctor, and at that instant she gave a final convulsive shiver and then relaxed.

The doctor stared at her, then straightened and looked across the bed at me.

"She is dead! For God's sake, what did you give her?"

CHAPTER XIX

I stood there, stupidly looking down at her. My own heart seemed to have stopped, and my mind, too. I was certainly not thinking.

"Wake up, woman! She's dead, I tell you. What was in the hypodermic?"

"What you ordered. You can look at the tube. You gave it to me yourself, Monday night."

"Bring that syringe here."

"I've washed it, doctor."

"Then bring me the tube. Bring in your tray."

His hands were shaking as he examined it, but he went over it carefully. There was not much on it; the usual morphia, but the tube containing it still sealed; the amyl-nitrite ampoules; some cotton and alcohol; and the nitroglycerin. One of these tablets he shook out in his hand and then put to his lips. Whatever he had expected to discover, he was evidently disappointed.

I was terribly frightened; more frightened than I had ever been in my life. I had not even time for pity. Every ounce of me was concentrated fiercely on self-protection.

"I gave her exactly what you ordered."

"How do I know you did? She's dead, and nitroglycerin didn't cause that spasm."

"I've never made such a mistake in my life!"

"Mistake or—something else."

"Good God, doctor! What do you think I gave her? Or why would I want to kill her?"

He made no reply to that. He came close to me, and I saw that his forehead was beaded with fine drops of perspiration. He got out his handkerchief and wiped it.

"Listen, Miss Adams," he said. "I believe that this unfortunate woman here has been poisoned. I don't know why, or by whom. I'm making no accusations. I'm not even certain of the fact. But I believe she was poisoned, with an alkaloidal poison of some sort."

"What sort?"

"Strychnia," he said grimly. "Strychnia. That's my guess, and it is yours."

"I don't know what you mean," I said wildly. "There's no strychnia on that tray."

"Not now." He put his handkerchief away, turned to the bed, and then faced me again.

"I prefer to say nothing more until I have called the police. You will remain in this room, please, until they arrive."

I tried to laugh, then. "And make me a prisoner! You can't mean that, doctor."

"I do mean it. And"—he added more slowly—"I begin to wonder if Hugo was right after all."

"What has Hugo to do with it?"

"He hasn't trusted you, for one thing. You can tell your story to the police when they get here, but I'll

174

say just this. I don't know what you are doing here. You were not my choice, if it comes to that. But Hugo has suspected all along that you were here for some purpose of your own. He has found you where you have had no business to be, and he wanted you sent off the case; he asked me to do that yesterday."

"I wish you had," I said bitterly. "I'd have been glad enough to go."

"That's as it may be. And I'll take that hypodermic, if you please. You were pretty quick about washing it!"

He slipped the case into his pocket, along with the other tube from the tray, and started out. But he hesitated at the door. His intention was clear enough; he wanted to lock me in. But he did not quite dare. I stood in the middle of the room and defied him.

"If you do that, doctor," I said clearly, "I shall shout for help from a window!"

He went out then, and in spite of that quiet old figure on the bed he slammed the door behind him. Then I could hear him running down the stairs, and shortly afterward, shouting at the telephone. He was trying to get through to the Inspector, who was evidently still closeted with the District Attorney. But he did get the Medical Examiner. I could hear that.

My anger had left me by that time. I went over to the bed, and looked down at the quiet figure lying there. Death had smoothed that terrible grin from Miss Juliet's face, so that now she looked younger, and very placid. I had no fear of the doctor's accusations, but I had a real regret for the method of her passing. Perhaps she had not had much time left, as she had said the night before; but little or much,

175

she had been entitled to it. And she had not seen her clergyman after all!

I was still dazed, of course. I made no move when the door opened, and Mary came in. She was not crying. Her face was a sort of bluish white, and she paid no attention to me whatever. She stood on the other side of the bed, looking down at the body, and then she did a queer thing. She made the sign of the cross over it, in the air. Only after that did she speak to me at all.

"Hugo's feeling poorly, miss. I said I'd tell you."

"You'd better get the doctor, Mary. He wants me to stay here."

She looked at me. "What's the use, now?" she said. "It's all over, isn't it? All over and done?"

"I'm afraid it's all over for Miss Mitchell, if that is what you mean."

She went out again, and I followed her to the landing. In the hall below, the doctor was pacing back and forth, his head sunk on his breast. He heard me, and told me sharply not to disturb anything; to leave the body alone, and the room. Then Mary told him about Hugo, and he went back with her toward the kitchen.

I suppose it was a half hour before the Medical Examiner got there, and with nothing to do I had plenty of time to think. I looked at Miss Juliet, lying so peacefully on her bed, and I had a bitter moment when I felt that, since she was to go, it was a pity that she had not gone before she signed Charlie Elliott's death warrant. For that it was, I knew. And now there would not even be the respite of a few days. Mr. Glenn would have to produce it, and at once.

176

It was only then that I began to see a possible connection between Miss Juliet's murder, if it was murder, and that confession. Suppose it had been intended that she never make that statement? Suppose someone, with access to that tray of mine, had skillfully plotted to kill her, so that it would never be signed?

I stood at the window, twisting a curtain cord in my hand, and tried to think that out. Who had had access to my tray recently? Recently, because I had already given her more than one hypodermic from that tube, with perfectly normal reactions. Hugo and Mary, of course, and even the doctor that morning, while I was downstairs getting water. And of course there had been Florence Lenz.

I thought about Florence. Had she been acting all the time, and was she really the blatant and rather disagreeable person she seemed to be? Or was there something else behind that frivolous manner of hers? Had she known Herbert Wynne? Would she have had any motive for putting Miss Juliet Mitchell out of the way? What lay behind her slipping into that room when she came upstairs? She had stood directly over the tray. It was covered with the powder she had been using. Wasn't it possible that that very powder was a sort of blind? Suppose she had been working over the tray, putting something into that nitroglycerin tube, when she heard me just outside?

We had come up the stairs very quietly. She could have had only a second or two of warning. Then what was more likely than a wild dash at my powder, spilling it in her excitement, in every direction?

But, once again, all of this was simply one of those

devices to which we all resort when we want to protect ourselves from some thought which is not bearable. I knew all along that I would have to come to Paula Brent.

She had hated Miss Juliet, and was convinced that she had had something to do with Herbert's death. Suppose that visit of hers that morning had been deliberately devised so that she could get into the house? The story of the letter an invention, and Paula determined that Miss Juliet, knowing something vital to Charlie Elliott's safety, should be put out of the way before she decided to talk?

She knew Doctor Stewart. She knew Mr. Glenn. Suppose the doctor had told her that Miss Juliet was being stimulated with nitroglycerin? Or the attorney had revealed that the old lady knew something, and was bound to tell it sooner or later? And the girl desperate, distracted.

I went back again over that little scene when the two girls met in my bedroom. There had been some deep and secret antipathy there. I had an idea that, while they had not met before, each knew about the other; and my mind once more went back to Herbert Wynne.

The Medical Examiner arrived while I was still standing there. I saw his gay little car come in, and he himself emerge, dapper as usual. I have sometimes thought that his bright car and his dandied dress were a sort of defense which he set up against what was often a gruesome business.

He was followed out of the car by a tall thin individual whom I recognized as the laboratory man from Headquarters. Doctor Stewart brought them both up, and the Medical Examiner seemed rather put out that the Inspector was not there.

"What makes you think it was poison?" he demanded.

"How would anybody know it? She was weak, but she wasn't dying. Then she gets these two hypodermics. She reacted very badly to the first, so I ordered a second."

"How far apart?"

"A half hour. The second caused the convu....on. There was *risus sardonicus*, very marked; and if you've ever seen angina cause that, you've seen more than I have."

The chemist had said nothing, but now he asked for the hypodermic and the tubes. He got them, handling them carefully and dropping them in an envelope, and then glanced at me. He knew me, but, like the Examiner, he made no sign that he did.

"Cleaned, I suppose?" He always spoke with a drawl, and now it seemed more marked than ever.

"Thoroughly. With alcohol."

"What do you think of this case?" he asked me.

Doctor Stewart glanced up angrily. "That's a question for the police, isn't it?"

"Oh, I don't know," he drawled. "After all, this young woman gave the stuff. She ought to know something, if there's anything to know."

"I think she was probably poisoned," I said quietly. "I don't know how it was done, but I venture to guess that, whatever was put into the nitroglycerin tube, whoever did it placed it there within the last twelve to fourteen hours. I had used nitroglycerin tablets before that, and they worked as they should."

179

He took out the tube, holding it in his handkerchief to do so, and, like the doctor, shook a tablet into his hand and put it to his tongue.

"No strychnia here, anyhow," he said. "Well, let's get busy, doctor."

"What will you want?" I asked.

"Nothing much. Some towels. We have everything else."

I shall not go into details of what followed. There was some talk of strychnia affecting the central nervous system, and so they took some spinal fluid as well as a specimen of blood from the jugular. I know that the laboratory man wanted the stomach, too, but he did not get it. The Medical Examiner wanted his lunch.

"Going to be hard enough to discover anything," said the laboratory man. "And even when these things are given by hypodermic, some of them resecrete in the stomach. Give us a chance."

"If you can't find it with what you've got, the chances are that it isn't there," said the Medical Examiner briefly, and drew off his rubber gloves.

The laboratory man lounged about the room while the other was preparing to go. He whistled softly as he moved, and Doctor Stewart eyed him without much favor. He was quite unconscious of it, however.

"Queer case, isn't it?" he drawled. "Here they have one murderer all safely locked away, and another one turns up!"

"If it *is* murder," said the Examiner, picking up his bag. "You get the idea of murder going, and you can see it everywhere. I'm still not sure that poor devil

180

upstairs didn't kill himself, last Monday night. He may have worked out something. You never can tell."

Then they went away, quite cheerfully. I could hear them arranging to lunch together as they went down the stairs. The tall man turned back to say that there would be a tentative report that night, but that it might take longer. I thought later that it was merely an excuse, for he leaned forward and said something in a low tone.

"Watch out for yourself, little lady," he said to me. "When these poison bugs get started, they don't know where to stop."

It was while Doctor Stewart was still below with them, and while I was cleaning the rubber sheet in the bathroom, that I heard a sound in Miss Juliet's room. I went to the door, to see Hugo on his knees beside the bed, his shoulders shaking. He got up when he heard me, and started out of the room, but he seemed unsteady as he walked. He had suddenly become an old man, a tired and feeble old man.

CHAPTER XX

It was after they had gone that the Inspector arrived. He said later that his car did not have to be steered any more; that it just naturally took the route to the Mitchell place and turned in there. And he took hold at once, hardly listening to the doctor's excited story.

"Examiner's been here already?" he asked. "Well, that's quick work. All right, Hugo. Go and sit down somewhere. And Miss Adams, I'll put you in charge of that room up there. Don't let anybody in. Now, doctor, if you'll come into the library, we'll talk this over."

"I protest against leaving Miss Adams in charge upstairs," said the doctor truculently.

Hugo had gone by that time, and the Inspector smiled at me and then patted me on the shoulder. "I know this young woman, doctor," he said. "It's perfectly safe to leave her here. Safe for us, anyhow. I'm not so sure about the lady!"

A chance statement which I was to remember with considerable bitterness a few hours later.

But the Inspector was not smiling when, a half

hour later, he came upstairs alone and into Miss Juliet's room. He closed the door behind him.

"I've sent Stewart off," he said. "He's an ass. A pompous little baldheaded ass! But he's pretty much worked up. I have an idea that he had hoped for a new will before she died, and this ends it. Don't let him worry you."

He glanced at me with a sort of half apology, and going to the bed, stood looking down at the sheeted figure on it.

"Life's a queer business, Miss Adams," he said, "but death is sometimes queerer. Now you take this old woman. Who would want to put her out of the way, if she *was* put out of the way? She hadn't long at the best."

"No. But she should have had that, at least."

"Precisely. She's got a little money. She's going to be comfortable and without worry. Then somebody decides to get rid of her, and—she's gone. Like that!"

"But she *is* gone," I pointed out. "We can't help her now; and you'll admit that Charlie Elliott had nothing to do with this. I take it he's still safely locked away?"

"He is, and he'll stay locked away."

"He hasn't talked, I suppose?"

"He talks all right, but he doesn't say anything. You heard him last night." He felt for his pipe, but after a look at the bed he took it out and held it, unfilled and unlighted, between his teeth.

"You know," he went on, "by and large I've seen a good bit of murder in my time, but this case gets me. We've got one suspect locked up, and this happens."

Well, I dare say my nerves had commenced to go,

184

for I found myself laughing, half hysterically.

"Maybe he did it, at that," I said, while he watched me carefully. "Maybe he wandered into my room last night on his way upstairs, and dropped a tablet or two into that tube on my tray. Why stop at one murder? He may have got a taste for it, like eating olives."

"You need a rest and a bromide," he said. "That is, if that's hysteria. If you're merely trying to be funny, for God's sake don't. I've had enough of it with that blond-haired killer at Headquarters. He'd better do his laughing now. He won't laugh long."

"You are as sure as that, are you, Inspector?"

"Sure enough."

"As sure as you were of suicide, and that scrap of paper?"

"What's that got to do with it? It was a week old. I've told you that."

"But it did have powder stains, didn't it?"

"Certainly it did. That doesn't necessarily mean anything. That was a pruning ladder that Paula Brent brought here that night, but she didn't prune any trees, did she?"

Well, I might have told him that there were two young men on the roof at that minute who had brought a ladder, too, but not to paint a roof. I refrained, however, for I saw that he was gravely troubled by the turn events had taken. He left the bed and moved about the room, and when he spoke again, it was in his usual businesslike manner.

"No use wasting time bickering over this case," he said. "You and I may not always see eye to eye, but we're likely to see a lot between us. I suppose you

185

agree with the doctor? It's poison, eh?"

"I think so, Inspector."

"And you've no idea how it got there?"

"I can think of a half-dozen ways. I'm not sure of any of them."

"Let's see where that tray was kept."

I led him into the other room, and he stood for some little time, surveying it. He opened the door into the hall, and glanced out.

"I suppose anybody could get in here. You didn't keep this door locked?"

"No."

I knew his methods. He preferred to get his own picture first, so I volunteered nothing. But he gave a quick look at my dresser, and then at my face.

"Who used the face powder? There's none on you."

Then I knew that the time had come to tell him of Miss Juliet's statement. I had dreaded it all along, but it had to come. We went back into Miss Juliet's room, and with that rigid thin old body on the bed, I told him my story.

I told of the article in the paper about Paula Brent, and its effect on Miss Juliet. I told of her bringing Mr. Glenn there the night before, and of the long argument and his protest, which had followed; and of Hugo's presence beside Miss Juliet's bed early that morning, before Mr. Glenn came, and his attitude of resentment.

"But she was determined to make that statement," I said. "She had something on her conscience, and she felt guilty. She wanted to make it, and then to see her clergyman."

He looked up quickly. "Why? Had she any idea

186

that there was trouble coming for her?"

"I think not."

"And Glenn has this statement now?"

"He took it away with him. Hugo and I witnessed it, and the Lenz girl, his secretary, is a notary. She attested it. But Miss Juliet didn't want it made public, Inspector. Mr. Glenn said—and she corroborated it—that it was only to be used in case a grave miscarriage of justice threatened. I suppose she was thinking of Paula Brent."

"You didn't read it, of course?"

"No. She folded it down, so none of us could see it."

"A grave miscarriage of justice, eh? Now what did that mean? I'll get hold of Glenn and have a look at it."

He left me then and went down to the telephone. I could hear him there, trying to locate either Florence or Mr. Glenn; but they were both out of the office at lunch, and Mr. Glenn had a case in court that afternoon. The Inspector came back in a very bad humor, having left word to trace them and get them to the Mitchell house as soon as possible. Then he went back to the kitchen and had a few words with Mary, and when he came back, his face was set.

I knew something had happened when I saw him. He stood for a moment, eying me coldly. "How many people have had access to that room of yours, and that tray, this morning?" he demanded. "The doctor, and the Lenz girl, and Hugo and Mary, I suppose. Is that all?"

"Don't use that tone with me, Inspector."

"Why didn't you tell me that Paula Brent was here

187

this morning? And that she was upstairs, at that!"

"I suppose Mary told you that."

"So she was upstairs? No, Mary didn't know that, but she saw her going out. Now listen to me, Miss Adams. Whether we see eye to eye on this case doesn't matter a damn. What does matter is that you decide whether you're working for me or for Paula Brent."

"She never poisoned Miss Juliet Mitchell, Inspector."

"Was she in that room?"

"Yes. But Florence Lenz was there at the same time."

It was only after I had said it that I remembered that Paula had been in that room later on as well, and alone. But he gave me no time to go on. He flushed angrily, and banged his hand on the arm of his chair.

"I'd break a man for doing a thing like that," he said. Then he relented, I suppose when he saw my face. "What story did she put up, to make you do a fool thing like that, and then keep it from me?"

"A story I believed. I still believe it, for that matter. And as for your breaking a man, you can break me and welcome. I'm about broken now anyhow. If I wasn't a darned fool, I'd be at home this minute, feeding sugar to my canary!"

That restored his temper, and he listened patiently while I told him Paula's story of the morning, and after some hesitation, that the keys they had found on Charlie Elliott were hers. But I did not tell him that Charlie Elliott had had those keys on Monday night. Why should I? Under oath I might have to, but not then.

"So she was going to Herbert's room!" he said.

"Well, I give up. One thing is certain, however. If Elliott had those keys later, he had them on Monday night, too. I imagine they are what our friend Henderson heard him taking from her. Well, we'll soon know."

He leaned back and started to light his pipe, but after a look at the bed he put it in his pocket.

"We'll soon know," he repeated. "But this morning is a horse of another color. So far as I can figure out, about six people have had access to that room of yours and that tray, in the last dozen hours or so: Hugo, Mary, Glenn, Paula Brent, Florence and Doctor Stewart.

"Hugo and Mary we know about. They had a motive and they had opportunity. But they were pretty loyal to the old lady. Glenn seems fairly well accounted for. He didn't want that statement made, but take the average man of his type, and he'll stand up for a boy like Charlie Elliott as against the law any time. If you think all lawyers are sold on the law, think again! Now take the doctor. What motive would *he* have? But the doctor, according to what you say, had a pretty good chance."

"He asked me last night about her will."

"Well, that's natural enough. She has left a good bit of money, and he knew she hadn't long."

"He said there was an old will, and that Hugo and Mary are left legacies in it."

"How much? Did he know?" he said quickly.

"He didn't say."

"I'll have a look at that will." He made a note in the small book he carries, and sat looking at it. "Both Hugo and Mary?"

189

"So he said."

"Well, let's get on. How about this Florence Lenz? I gather you don't like her."

"I don't."

"Why?"

"I know her type, and I don't like it," I said shortly. "She's playing up to Mr. Glenn, for one thing. Rolls her stockings and lets him know it. And she staged a faint here that night when she was scared in the grounds. It wouldn't have fooled anybody. It didn't fool me, anyhow."

He began that sort of noiseless whistling which often accompanies his thinking, and slid farther down in his chair.

"Of course," he said finally, "in a way, poison is a woman's method. She isn't strong enough to use a knife, and it's messy anyhow. She hates blood. In a majority of cases she's afraid of firearms. But poison is different. She can understand poison. I don't suppose you can connect this Florence with the case?"

"I'm not certain. I think she hates Paula Brent, but I don't know why."

I told him then about the encounter that morning, and he listened carefully.

"It was Florence who was the aggressor?"

"Yes. But Paula Brent knew her, or knew who she was. She was almost rude, herself."

He looked at his watch. "Well, the Lenz woman ought to be here soon. It would be interesting to find out whether she knew Herbert, or this Elliott boy. In that case . . ." He shifted to something else. "How about Mary? She's been taking strychnia for her

190

heart, if this was strychnia. But in capsules, not hypodermic tablets. She's a queer woman, fanatically religious, according to the doctor, and neurotic. But sane enough."

"She cleaned my room this morning."

"Well, you dressed in it probably. That doesn't mean you killed this poor old woman, does it? No. Take it all in all, Miss Pinkerton, and what does this second murder look like? For I think it was murder. What happens when any crime is committed? The first step is to escape and leave nothing incriminating behind. The next step, once the escape is made, is to protect that escape.

"That is, the murderer's fear is not for the thing he knows about and can clear up, but for the thing that turns up later on. He lies awake at night and worries about that. The somebody or something which he hasn't counted on, and which may destroy him.

"Now take this case. Here's the way it looks just now. I'm not saying it's right. Herbert Wynne was killed last Monday night, and we think we have the killer. We have every reason to think so. But here is Miss Juliet hiding something, and finally deciding to spill it. Something damaging to the killer, of course. That has to be suppressed, or at least the old lady put where she can't confirm it on the stand, we'll say. So she is poisoned."

He looked at me. "I would give a good bit to know," he said, "just how many people knew in advance that she was going to make that statement. Did this Florence?"

"She seemed to think it was a will. That is, until Mr. Glenn explained."

191

"Well, Hugo knew; and probably Mary. But maybe not. I have an idea that he isn't very communicative with her."

"She may have known. I found her listening outside the door this morning."

"The doctor didn't know, did he?"

"I think not. But I've just thought of something. I don't believe two hypodermics of strychnia, say, a fifteenth of a grain in each, would have killed or hurt most people. It was only in her condition that it was fatal."

He sat up and stared at me. "It wasn't a poisonous dose in itself?"

"I couldn't buy a hypodermic tablet of strychnia that would be poisonous in itself, unless I wanted to use it on a horse! And I want to ask you something, now. Paula Brent says that there was a letter left in Herbert's room, and if the people here haven't got it, it is still there. Have you ever given that room upstairs a real search? One based on the conviction that something is really hidden there?"

"I've been over it. You know that."

"Then go over it again," I said half hysterically. "Go up the chimney, or tear off the floor boards. Look around that bed. I tell you there was something else. It may be gone, but it was there. And I think it will solve these crimes."

It was at that moment that the doorbell rang, and Hugo announced Florence Lenz.

192

CHAPTER XXI

I was not present at the Inspector's interview with Florence. I could hear her in the lower hall, loudly explaining that she had notified Mr. Glenn and that he would be here as soon as court adjourned; and from the delay there I fancied that she had stopped as usual before the mirror to make up her face.

That must have irritated him, for I heard his voice, sharp and edged.

"Come, come, Miss Lenz," he said. "This isn't a beauty parlor."

"I'll say it isn't!"

She flounced into the library, or so I imagined, and he closed the door.

I had nothing to do for the next half hour or so but to worry. I had been told not to touch anything in the room, and so far the press had apparently not been notified of the death. But it does not take long for such news to get about, and as I looked out of the window, I saw the usual car driving in through the old gates, and the usual young man with a soft hat and businesslike manner getting out of it.

Hugo answered the bell, and I called to him softly

as he went through the hall, telling him to give simply the facts of the death, and the hour. It must have been two o'clock by that time, or even later. I had had no luncheon, and Mary had apparently retired to her room and locked herself in. But soon after that, Hugo rapped at my door with some crackers and milk. He did not look at the bed as he crossed the floor.

"My wife is ill, miss," he said. "I'm sorry. She'll get up to cook dinner."

"What about that reporter, Hugo?"

"I did as you said, miss."

He looked inscrutable to me, seen in the strong afternoon light that day. Old and suddenly feeble, but inscrutable. On an impulse I followed him as he turned to go, and put my hand on his arm.

"She's gone, Hugo," I said. "Perhaps she didn't need to go so soon, but—well, she's gone. Why not tell all you know. You will feel better for it, and she would have wanted it."

"She has told it, miss," he said heavily. "She told it this morning."

The Inspector called me down soon after that. Florence was still in the room, dabbing at her eyes with her handkerchief, and the Inspector's face was stern but not unkind.

"I think we have got to the bottom of some of this, Miss Adams," he said. "This young woman was at one time engaged to Herbert Wynne, or so she claims."

"I was," she broke in, but he raised a hand for silence.

"This engagement, however, was broken last

March, and she had not seen him since. But she knew that he was being seen constantly with Paula Brent. That explains her attitude to Miss Brent when they met today.

"This morning she came to the house with Mr. Glenn, to attest what she had expected to be a will. She waited downstairs until sent for; then something additional was apparently to be added to Miss Juliet's statement, and she was left in the hall. From there she went into your room for face powder, and she was there when you brought Paula Brent in. Miss Brent left the room soon after that.

"Following that, she went with you into the large bedroom to witness the statement, and did so. But on leaving that room to go back to the office with Mr. Glenn, she opened the door into the upper hall, and she says she saw Miss Brent again. She was going into your room."

"That is true, Inspector," I said. "I found her there. She had been to the third floor, and as someone was in the hall, she couldn't get out. She didn't want to be seen."

"Why didn't you tell me this before?"

"Because it is absurd to suspect Paula Brent of poisoning anybody."

And at that, that vixen in the corner let out a yelp of laughter, and I could cheerfully have killed her.

"How do you know she had been to the third floor?"

"I should know," I said with some bitterness. "She's been trying to get there all week, and you know it."

"Faithful, wasn't she?" Florence jeered. "Well, I'm

on my way if that's all, Inspector. Bye-bye! Be good!"

The Inspector let her go without a word, and I was just bracing myself for a defense when Mr. Glenn's car drove up. That saved me for the time, although, by the very manner in which the Inspector told me that I could go, I realized that his faith in me was pretty thoroughly shaken.

Mr. Glenn breezed in a moment later, and I knew well enough what that meant.

As I went up the stairs, I was determined to get off the case and out of the house. I was heartsick and homesick. I wanted to get back to my little apartment, and see Dick's eyes when I went to the closet for sugar. I wanted to sleep for twenty-four hours.

It may sound funny now to say that, when the Inspector came up, I was packing my bag to go, and that I had put on my hat, although I still wore a uniform. It was not funny then. That impulse to get out was nothing but a premonition; I know that now. I had not a doubt in the world that day but that Charlie Elliott would go to the chair, and I was not so certain that Paula would not go with him.

I heard Mr. Glenn going, and the Inspector coming up the stairs. He walked heavily, like a tired man, and when he came into my room, I even thought that, like Hugo, he looked older. He sat down without saying anything, and got out his pipe and lighted it.

"I dare say it's bad news?" I asked.

"I suppose that depends on the point of view. It doesn't cover everything, but it covers enough. I suppose you'd like to read it. You certainly deserve to get the low-down on this case, if anyone does."

Which I took to be his apology. After all, he could afford to be lenient; he had his case in his pocket, and he knew it. He produced the statement and passed it to me, and well enough I knew it; Mr. Glenn's careful writing, Miss Juliet's signature, my own signature in the corner, then Hugo's, and below them Florence's seal.

"You'll find," he said, "that the early portion of the story is substantially as Miss Juliet told it before. It is only at the end that it differs."

But I read it from start to finish nevertheless, with a slowly sinking heart. Clearly she had dictated it in her own words, although here and there was the evidence of a legal mind.

"I, Juliet Mitchell, being of sound mind and in the full possession of my faculties, wish to make the following statement, which I hereby state is the truth and nothing but the truth. I say this realizing that before long I shall have to face my Maker.

"My previous testimony to the police was also true to a certain extent. It is true that, on the night of Monday, September the fourteenth, I was awakened at about ten minutes before twelve by someone passing outside my door, and looked at my clock. It is true that I then prepared to go up the stairs to see if my nephew had come home, and that while preparing to get out of bed I felt by the vibration of the floor that someone was passing in the hall. It is true that on going to my door and seeing the light burning in his room above, I called to him and received no answer. And it is also true that I then put on my dressing gown and slippers and went up to his room to put out the light."

197

Here, however, this rather formal style ended, and Miss Juliet began to tell her story in a more ordinary manner, and to this effect:

She had got halfway up the stairs that night, from which point her head was slightly above the floor level above, and she could see directly into the room. To her horror, she saw her nephew lying on the floor in the center of the room, not moving.

What followed, according to that statement, must have had for her the stark drama of a silent motion picture shown in a dark theater. She could hear nothing, of course, and the brilliantly lighted room must have been like a stage, seen through the open door. However that may be, she was clear enough as to what followed. From a space which she could not see, but which was apparently the location of the closet or the bed, she saw a man approach this body and stoop over it; a young man, fair-haired and well dressed. To her horror, she then saw him drag what she now realized was Herbert's dead body toward the dresser; and stooping again, saw him deliberately bend the legs and lay a revolver beside it.

Up to that moment the full import of what she was seeing had not dawned on her. But with this man still stooping, she had found her breath and began to shriek. The figure turned and looked toward her, and then made a leap toward the window. Whether he escaped that way or not she was not certain. As she had only gone down the stairs to arouse the servants, however, he couldn't have passed her. She was convinced that he had gone by way of the roof.

But, although she had recognized the guilty man, she did not tell either Hugo or Mary when they appeared, and Hugo had at first believed that it was suicide. Also, Hugo had said that if it was suicide, it would invalidate certain insurance policies held by Herbert, and suggested moving the body away from the bureau. But this she would not allow. She was back on the stairs again at that time, with Mary holding aromatic ammonia to her nose. She had not been able to climb all the way to the room.

It was Hugo who discovered that there were no powder marks around the wound, and called to her that it was either a murder or accidental death. There was some unimportant detail here, and then Miss Juliet entered into a defense of her course of action which was typical and yet almost incredible. She went on to state that she had given Herbert a home, and what she could of support, and he had rewarded her with cold ingratitude. She would not pretend, even now, that she felt any grief at his death, or that the world had suffered any loss. And she was entirely engrossed that night, she admitted, with the situation in which she found herself.

There had never been a scandal of this sort in the Mitchell family. They had made their mistakes, but if Herbert had been murdered, she was convinced that it had been for good and sufficient reason. She dreaded the publicity, the stirring up of some filth— the word is mine—which would disgrace what had been a proud old name, and she was prepared to take any steps possible to avoid this.

Also there was another reason. She had recognized the boy. He belonged to a good family, and had at one time been engaged to Paula Brent, the granddaughter of an old friend of hers. She had made up her mind, sitting weakly there on the stairs that night, to keep her knowledge to herself!

She broke off here, to say that she did not know when or where Hugo had opened a window downstairs. She learned later that one had been found open; and she believed that he had done so in his anxiety to prove the case not one of suicide. He had been a loyal employee, and he knew that there was some insurance. Nor did she know when he had sent for the police. She herself had asked him to telephone to Mr. Glenn, and he had arrived shortly after the police got there. But she had had no chance to talk to him that night. Mary had sent for Doctor Stewart, and he had ordered her to bed.

Then she went back to her story. It was much later on Monday night, toward morning, indeed, that, as she lay in her bed, it had occurred to her that this man was probably still on the roof and unable to escape. She had felt fairly safe until then; Mary had reported that the police thought it was either suicide or accidental death, and probably an accident. But if he was still on the roof, it meant discovery, so she got out of bed and went upstairs. She leaned out of the window and called to him, but he must have escaped, for he did not answer to his name.

That name was Charlie Elliott.

CHAPTER XXII

There was more of it, but nothing of importance. All the week, it was evident, Miss Juliet had struggled with an increasing sense of sin. She believed in the Bible, and there was the law of an eye for an eye, a tooth for a tooth. She had allowed her pride and a sentiment for an old friend to defeat the law, God's law and man's. It was when she learned that Herbert had taken out a large amount of insurance, and that his death had released her from serious financial worry, that she began to see where her duty lay.

She could not profit by his murder and protect his murderer; if, indeed, it were a murder. And when she saw by the paper that Paula Brent had been dragged into the case, she determined to do what she should have done at once.

It was that astounding document, which meant the chair for that blithe boy who had faced us all down that night in that upper room, which Hugo and I had signed. Here was Miss Juliet's wavering signature, here was Hugo's shaking one, and my own scrawl.

I stood, holding it in my hand and gazing at nothing. So Paula had known all along that Miss

Juliet had seen Charlie in the room, and that the old lady could destroy him with a word. Here was Florence, telling the police Paula had gone back to my room that morning; had been there alone. Inspector Patton was watching me, a curious look on his face.

"Now you know what I've been talking about," he said. "I don't claim that I knew the old lady had seen Elliott in that room. But I do claim that I've known all along that Paula Brent knew more than she was telling. Then what do you do? You go out of your way, and forget your duty into the bargain, to tell her that Miss Mitchell is about to confess something! And I'll tell you something maybe you don't know. Paula's in love with this Elliott boy. Maybe she doesn't know it either, but that's the fact. It sticks out like a sore thumb. She's in love, and she's desperate."

"How could she know I was giving that Nitroglycerin?"

"Well, that's not hard, is it? Maybe you told her; you seem to have told her a good bit, one way and another. Maybe Doctor Stewart told her; he's the family doctor for the Brents. Maybe she got into your room on Tuesday night and saw your tray. As a matter of fact, maybe that's why she got into the house. I don't uphold that theory. I only mention it."

"I've given half a dozen hypodermics since then."

"Still, she might have seen what you were using. And there were only two tubes on that tray. One of them was morphia, and it had not been opened. The other was nitroglycerin. Just remember that."

"And I suppose Paula Brent knew what was the matter with Miss Juliet's heart! And what it could

202

stand, or couldn't!"

But I was remembering something else. "Listen, Inspector," I said earnestly. "You couldn't buy strychnia in hypodermic tablets so that two would be a poisonous dose. If those two injections killed Miss Juliet, that was because of her heart condition. Whoever substituted those tablets must have known that. Do you think a girl like Paula Brent could possibly have known such a thing?"

"You're certain of that, are you?"

"Ask the doctor."

He was silent for a few minutes, evidently turning that over in his mind. Then he got up and wandered to the bureau, standing in front of it and surveying it with care: my silver brush and comb; the tray, looking strangely empty and useless; my box of powder. With his back to me, he spoke again.

"I suppose you wouldn't notice if the tube had been tampered with?"

"It was a fresh tube. I had opened it, but I had not used it."

He wheeled. "A fresh tube? Then, supposing two tablets had been put into it, two others would have had to come out."

"Yes. Although I hadn't thought of it."

He looked around then. The bathroom, as in most old houses, was reached only by way of the hall. He glanced at the carpet, got down to examine some powder Florence had spilled on the floor, found it only powder, and then, rising, glanced at the rear window, which was open.

"What about that window? Was it open all morning?"

"It was."

"Let me see one of those tablets."

"The laboratory man took them."

He muttered something, and then, without another word, he went out of the room and down the stairs.

I looked at my watch, and I had to hold it to my ear to be certain that it had not stopped. It was only a little after four, and it seemed to me that I had lived a lifetime since morning. The house was as still as only a house with death in it can be. There was no sign of Hugo, or of Mary; but from the rear window of mine I could see Mary's black cat, moving stealthily across the grass toward the building. When I went closer to the window, I saw what had attracted it. The Inspector was furiously moving that ladder from where I had thrown it, and loudly demanding to know how it had got there!

Well, it had been a bad day for me, and was slowly growing worse. And evidently the two youths on the roof felt rather the same, for they never peeped while he was below.

He flung the ladder away, and then began to go over the ground with minute care, getting down on his hands and knees to do so. His tall figure in its gray sack suit was concentration personified, and I drew my first real breath when I saw him pick up some small object, lay it in the palm of his hand, and then drop it lightly in one of those small glass vials which the Bureau provides for such purposes.

But when I turned away from that window, I knew one thing, and knew it beyond a doubt. Miss Juliet had been murdered; deliberately and skillfully murdered.

The Inspector did not find the other tablet, apparently. Or he was satisfied with the one. I heard him coming back into the house, and up the stairs. But he made no explanation to me. He passed my door as though I were not in the room, and moving with that peculiar catlike rapidity which is his when he needs it, he went on up the third-floor stairs and into Herbert's room.

Some ten minutes later he was down again, and at my door. "Can you get me a hammer?" he said. "One with a tack puller on the other end, or something of the sort?"

"There is a drawer of tools in the pantry. But I imagine Hugo is there."

"Then don't try it." He scanned the room quickly. "Have you a nail file, or a strong pair of scissors?"

Well, I had both, and I gave them to him. "They are my best surgical scissors," I told him. "Don't break them."

"My God!" he said. "What a contradictory person you are, Miss Pinkerton! You go calmly through murder and sudden death, and now you don't want your scissors broken. Take that hat off and stop being ridiculous! And if Hugo shows up, ask for something from downstairs. Tea, molasses, I don't care what. Just hold him."

He was excited; I could see that. He is seldom facetious except at such times. Excited and happy, like a dog which has followed a cold trail for a long time, and suddenly finds it a hot one.

"I gather that you found something, down below that window."

"I did," he said dryly. "I found that a hardhearted

205

young woman had left a couple of reporters on a hot tin roof, and that it is only by the grace of Providence that in venting her personal spleen she didn't destroy some valuable evidence."

He grinned at me, and then he was on his way upstairs again, taking the steps two or three at a time."

He was upstairs for some fifteen minutes. Then I heard him coming down, and at the same time Hugo's slow steps on the staircase, coming up. They met just outside my door, and neither one of them seemed to realize that I was there. I can still see Hugo, stopping and looking up, and the Inspector moving down on him, stern and implacable.

But it was Hugo who spoke first. "I was going to ask about the funeral arrangements. I suppose we can go ahead with them?"

"Why not?"

"You know that better than I do, sir. But if she died a natural death, why bring the Medical Examiner? You don't think she did; nor I either." Then, without any warning, he broke down and began to weep, the terrible unwilling tears of age. To weep and to talk. "I killed her, Inspector. I'd have done anything for her, and—I killed her!"

"Pull yourself together, Hugo," the Inspector said sharply. "You are not confessing a crime to me, are you?"

But Hugo only shook his head, and would have passed on. The Inspector caught him by the shoulder.

"Why don't you come clean about this?" he said.

"What's the use now, Hugo? She's gone."

"I have nothing to say, sir."

"You've said something already, too much or too little."

"I've got my wife to think of, Inspector. If anything happens to me, what will become of her?"

"What could happen to you?" the Inspector demanded roughly. "I know about the insurance, and your fear that Herbert's death would be considered a suicide. I know that you wanted to move the body away from the bureau up there, for that reason. And I understand that better than you think. But I know a lot of other things also. For instance, why Miss Juliet got out of bed that night and went up to the room again."

"She told that, sir?"

"She did."

"It was my fault that she didn't do it before, sir."

The Inspector nodded. He still had his hand on Hugo's shoulder.

"Isn't it time you told what you know, Hugo? Or what you suspect? What's the use of holding back now? If you're afraid, I'll take steps to protect you."

"Protect me! You couldn't protect *her*, sir."

"But if I tell you that I know the whole story? What then?"

Hugo did not answer. He caught hold of the stair rail, looked blankly ahead of him, and then crumpled up on the floor in a dead faint.

It was some little time before he recovered sufficiently to be moved from my room, where the Inspector had carried him, and still later before he was strong enough to be taken to Headquarters for interrogation. Up to the time he left, he had

207

stubbornly refused to talk, and much of that time the Inspector had spent in pacing up and down in the lower hall. I had gone down to the kitchen and on up the back stairs to tell Mary, but although she was clearly startled, it was some time before I could induce her to open the door and let me in.

She was not in bed. She had apparently been sitting by the window, and she was fully dressed. She was pale, even for her, and I had to assure her that I was alone before she would unlock the door. She was suspicious even then, for she kept looking over my shoulder into the sitting room.

"Where is he?" she asked.

"In my room, Mary."

Then, for the first time that day, so far as I knew, she broke down and cried.

I took her to Hugo, and she bent down and touched his forehead with her work-hardened hand.

"I told you," she said. "I told you. But you're a stubborn man."

He opened his eyes and looked at her, and I saw then that, whatever had separated them, there was a strong bond between them; the bond of years and habit, and maybe something more. He took her hand.

"My poor Mary," he said weakly. "My poor girl."

It was about that time that the Inspector ordered the release of the two boys on the roof. Instead of leaving at once, however, I saw them in deep conference with the Inspector in the lower hall. One of them had something in his hand, and the Inspector took it and looked at it.

I could not see what it was.

CHAPTER XXIII

The reporters had barely gone, to the sound of considerable badinage from one or two cameramen in the drive, when the doorbell rang.

That was nothing new that afternoon. The neighbors, the Manchesters and the Bairds, had already heard our news, by that sort of grapevine telegraph which travels from kitchen to kitchen, and had called to offer condolences and help. Indeed, it had been all I could do to keep Mrs. Manchester from settling in the house that afternoon.

"There should be a woman around," she said, looking at me with wide protruding eyes.

"I am here. And Mary."

"Mary!" she said with a sniff.

So I expected a reporter, or a neighbor, when I opened the door. But it was Mr. Henderson who stood on the front porch. Apparently he had already learned of Miss Juliet's death, for he had his hat in his hand, and he tiptoed in after the manner of most people in a house of death, and spoke with his voice decorously lowered.

"Is Inspector Patton here?" he half whispered.

"I've been to Headquarters, and they said he was here."

The Inspector emerged from the darkness of the rear hall.

"I'm here, Henderson. Want to see me?"

"I don't like to intrude at a time like this, but my wife felt that I should see you. Perhaps if we could go outside and talk . . ."

"Speak right up. It's all right."

"Well, it's like this." He stood turning his hat in his hands and hesitating. "I don't like to repeat gossip myself. Live and let live is my motto. But Mrs. Henderson has a way of receiving people's confidence. You'd be surprised how much she hears. And lately she has learned something about Paula Brent. It seems that our cook is friendly with the Brent's butler, and she has a sort of cock-and-bull story that my wife thinks you ought to know."

Well, it was just one of those things that might be important, or might be simply backstairs talk. As the Inspector said after Henderson left, "I've got an idea that that henpecked little man, as well as his wife, has been holding an opera glass on those two houses across the alley ever since the murder."

But stripped of his apologies and so on, it ran as follows:

According to this butler, about a month before, Paula Brent had gone to a house party. But something turned up over that weekend, and when her family called her by long distance, they found that she was not there. On Sunday night she came home, in her car, and according to the butler there was a terrific scene. Her father shouted and raved like

210

a madman, and one of the things he said was overheard. He said, "If I find out who the man is, I'll kill him."

Paula was crying, and so was her mother; and apparently they locked her up that night in her own room. She was locked up for two days. The servants were told that she was ill, but no one entered her room but her mother, and she carried in Paula's trays. She ate little or nothing, however. The trays went down practically as they went up.

"I didn't much care about reporting this," said the little man, "but as a decent citizen I suppose I should." He seemed to draw a long breath. "Mr. Brent is a good friend and a good neighbor. We're on the School Board together. Of course it is Mrs. Henderson's idea that if Mr. Brent had anything to do with all this, he had justification. But she has just heard of Miss Juliet's death, and what with Charlie Elliott locked up and all——"

The Inspector looked up sharply. "So that's the talk, is it?"

Mr. Henderson spread his hands. "You can't keep people from talking, Inspector. Mrs. Henderson heard that Miss Juliet was dead, and she called the Brent house . But it was Paula who came to the telephone, and my wife says she never said a word. Just hung up the receiver. My wife was pretty much upset about it."

"What are they saying about Miss Juliet's death?"

"I didn't listen to it all. But Doctor Stewart called on Mrs. Brent this afternoon, and I believe the butler heard something."

"Something? What?"

"Well, the doctor seemed to feel that the death wasn't natural."

"Oh, damn the doctor!" said the Inspector, with feeling. "And why in God's name would Mr. Brent do away with Miss Juliet Mitchell?"

The little man cleared his throat. "It's my wife's idea that possibly—well, suppose the old lady found Paula Brent in that room that night, as well as Charlie Elliott?"

"*And* Paula's father. Quite a crowd, wasn't it?"

He spread his hands. "I don't think that, Inspector. I'm only telling you the talk in our neighborhood."

"Well, go home and tell them to shut up," said the Inspector savagely. "I don't need any help on this case; when I do, I'll ask for it."

The little man creaked out soon after that, and the Inspector remained thoughtful when he had shut the door behind him. He did not speak again until we were both in the library with the door closed, and he was methodically filling his pipe.

"Funny thing," he said, "how the public clamors for a victim, isn't it? Brent was out of town last Monday night; and I don't mean maybe."

He took a turn up and down the hall. "What do you make of all this?" he asked suddenly.

"I think," I said dryly, "that when Miss Juliet died, the defense lost an important witness. And that somebody knew it."

"A witness for the defense! Now that's interesting. Why?"

"The old lady didn't claim to have seen the shot fired, did she? All she saw was the boy in the room."

"She saw him moving the body."

"How do you know that? I'd give a good bit to know if she had taken time that night to put on her distance glasses! She couldn't see across a room without them."

He was watching me, with that unblinking gaze of his.

"And how about this gossip we've just listened to? Suppose young Elliott hadn't known about that excursion a month ago, and just heard it, last Monday night?"

"Well," I said stubbornly, "I don't know anything about this young generation, and thank God I'm not its moral censor. But I'll never believe Charlie Elliott is guilty of that murder."

He had been moving uneasily about the room. Now he took his pipe from his mouth and grinned at me.

"You're an obstinate young woman, Miss Pinkerton," he said. "But you've got a certain amount of common sense, along with your weakness for blond youths! And I'll admit that several things today have me out on a limb, and with no Paula Brent to come along with a ladder. That old woman was poisoned; I don't need a laboratory report to tell me that."

"You found the tablets?"

"I found one of them. That's good enough. If it hadn't been for your vindictive act with that ladder, I'd probably have both of them."

"That ought to let Charlie Elliott out," I said, with a certain relief. But he merely sucked at his pipe and followed his own line of thought.

"Now we have two murders. The first one is a case for the Grand Jury; no doubt about that. The D. A.

213

has young Elliott in a barrel with the lid nailed on. He's out for an indictment, and he'll get it as sure as God made little fishes. But I want no miscarriage of justice, and there isn't a doubt that if our little friend Henderson goes on the stand with his story of last Monday night in that alley, it's a case of just too bad for Charlie Elliott. What he took from Paula Brent that night was probably her bag, with the keys to this house in it.

"But I've been lying awake at night over this whole affair, and it puzzles me. A furiously jealous man commits a crime of passion. He's out to kill, and he does it. He's not a calculating human being; he doesn't fire a shot while holding a revolver in his handkerchief, and then set the stage to look like a suicide. For one thing, there isn't time. A shot isn't like a knife wound. It makes a devil of a lot of noise. Then, here's this statement of Miss Juliet's that he moved the body. Maybe you're right, and she imagined that. But it will send this boy to the chair just the same."

"There is another thing, Inspector. How did he know that shot wouldn't be heard? He probably knew that Miss Juliet was deaf, but what about the servants? I don't believe he had ever been in this house before. Whoever fired that shot either took a long chance that it wouldn't be heard, or—knew that it wouldn't."

"Meaning Hugo, I suppose?"

"Hugo knew about it. Or knows about it. I haven't watched him all week for nothing."

He nodded, and smoked in silence for some little time.

"Just what do you know about this Florence Lenz?" he asked.

"Nothing, except that she's a hussy."

He threw back his head and laughed. But he sobered almost at once. "Nevertheless, hussy or no hussy," he said, "it might be important to find out, for example, if she knew by any chance that Paula Brent had married Herbert Wynne."

"What?" I screeched. "Married him!"

"She did, indeed," he said gravely. "She has kept her secret pretty well, but that accounts for that weekend excursion of hers. It's a pity we can't see the Henderson woman's face when she learns it, isn't it? Yes, she married him, and one of the things she has been trying to get from this house is her wedding certificate, poor child. I have a suspicion that she knew that marriage had been a mistake, even before he was killed. But that's what she did, and—if it relieves your mind—that is why she carried those keys."

"But why break in for that certificate? I don't understand. Surely she didn't need a certificate to prove the marriage?"

"I've been thinking it over, and the only explanation I have is that they were married at night, possibly in some remote place he had selected, and that she was excited or frightened, and didn't even know where it was done."

"Where did you find it? The certificate? I suppose you have found it?"

"I did, and by the way, I owe you a new pair of surgical scissors. It was behind the baseboard at the head of the bed. Herbert had ripped off the molding and dropped it there. I had the devil of a time fishing it out."

"And there was no letter?" I asked.

"There was a letter, but it doesn't tell us much. I'll come to that in due time. Let's keep on with this girl, Paula. Now, if she had done the normal thing, she'd have told that at the start. But few of us do the normal thing when we're frightened, and she was pretty thoroughly scared. For one thing, while she didn't believe young Elliott had killed Herbert Wynne, she wasn't sure. She isn't sure even now. She only has his word for it. And she was in dead wrong with her people. For whatever reason, Wynne wanted that marriage kept secret; the minute he died, she wanted that certificate to show her people. But it's a curious bit of psychology that people in trouble always believe that the police are against them. We'd have turned up that preacher for her, but does she tell us? She does not.

"Let's follow her a bit. She's in trouble, all right. On Tuesday night she gets into this house and scares you into a fit. Scares herself, too! On Wednesday she tells Charlie Elliott the whole story, and he makes a try, but Florence runs him off the place. And on Thursday he finally makes the grade, and we get him. He may be guilty of the murder; guilty as hell. Or he may be as innocent as an unborn babe. But we've got him."

"But the letter!" I said impatiently. "Doesn't that tell anything?"

"It does and it doesn't. I'm not going into that too far just now. But I'll tell you this. The whole thing started as an insurance swindle, and nothing else.

216

He—Herbert—was to take out a considerable sum of straight life insurance. It is cheap at his age; and the idea was to arrange a drowning; or rather a pseudo-drowning. It was his own scheme at first. He wanted a lump sum for carrying it out; enough to get away, and a payment later to make a start somewhere else. He went to Hugo with it, and at first Hugo refused. Then he agreed, I suppose, for two reasons. It would provide for the old lady in her need, and it would ensure his legacy, and Mary's.

"But here's the devil of it. Hugo gave him the money for the premiums, either from his own savings or borrowed elsewhere. He didn't know, and in the end it was Hugo this boy was afraid of. You see, he had held up the plan, and Hugo didn't like it. Miss Juliet was about to lose her home.

"He had got his advance money, and he had gone into the market with it. But the market had gone down, and he didn't want to 'die' until he could get his money out again, and a little more. For by that time he had met Paula Brent, and fallen in love with her. You can see how it was; the boy keeps postponing the date of his pretended death by drowning. The summer goes by, the obvious time for such a trick, and still he hasn't done it. What's more, he is apparently stalling. He's fallen in love, and it looks as though he might quit the game. Hugo takes to watching him, and he knows that he's out with this girl at night a good bit.

"What's more, he may marry her! That is fatal to the scheme; his wife becomes his heir, and not the old lady. That's why Herbert hid the certificate and swore Paula to secrecy, although I doubt if the girl knew anything about the plot. And no wonder he was rather cheery on that last night! He could pull that drowning as before, but Paula would get the money. They could ship off to Europe or South America, and live happily ever after. Only he waited a day or two too long."

"And Hugo murdered him, after all?"

"I haven't said that, have I?" he said. He got up and shook the ashes out of his pipe. "If Glenn gets here within an hour or so, tell him to call me up, will you? I'm taking Hugo with me. And here's a last thought for you. Suppose the Lenz girl knew about this plot, and expected to marry him and share the profits? It's an interesting idea, isn't it?"

But I noticed that he had told me nothing about what those two reporters had found on the roof.

CHAPTER XXIV

When I went upstairs again, the morticians, as they call themselves now, had been at work for some time in Miss Juliet's room, and soon after, they called me in to look at her. All traces of her sickness and trouble had disappeared, and she lay, like an old marble statue, in her wide walnut bed. They had put a little color on her face and arranged the lights, and when they called me in, I was almost startled. She had become the great lady again, majestic and almost beautiful. It was not hard to believe that she had once been a beauty, and that Paula Brent's grandfather had been passionately in love with her.

Mr. Glenn did not arrive until five o'clock, and I gave him the Inspector's message. He called up at once, and I heard him saying that something was in Miss Juliet's box at the bank, and that he would locate it in the morning.

Hugo had not returned, and I was glad that there was someone in the house besides Mary, strangely set and brooding in her kitchen. For the afternoon papers had carried the notice of Miss Juliet's death, and almost immediately people had commenced to arrive. They came in numbers and dignity, these elderly folk, some merely leaving their cards, others coming in. Some arrived in cars, but here and there was an ancient victoria, used only for ceremonial occasions, and driven by an equally ancient coachman in shabby livery. When they came in, it was with the careful movements and the lowered voices proper to such occasions. Old gentlemen leaning on sticks, elderly woman rustling after the fashion of years ago, they came and went, a little sad, a little alarmed; for the death of the aged was to most of them a warning that they themselves had not long to live, that soon the same decorous gathering would be for them.

Almost none of them asked to see the old lady.

I was rather surprised, however, to find Mr. Henderson among those who did so. Led by the doctor, he came up and stood by the bed, in silence at first.

"Knew her when I was a boy," he said jerkily. "They say she grew hard, but she wasn't hard then. Beautiful, she was."

He tiptoed out on creaking shoes, but as he went, he gave a sharp look at the stairs to the third floor.

"It's a pity she didn't go before *that* happened," he said.

I was surprised to see tears in his eyes as he creaked down the stairs again. I have often thought of him since, that little man; finding his bit of romance vicariously in the Miss Juliets and the Paula Brents, and living his drab suppressed existence with the woman he always referred to as "my wife."

And we were not through with him. I was to see him once more before anonymity closed down on him, and that under strange and tragic circumstances.

Rather to my surprise Hugo was back and served the dinner that night. Mr. Glenn paid little attention to him, being apparently absorbed in his own thoughts. But once, when Hugo was out of the room, he spoke about him.

"Looks pretty well broken," he said. "Aged, don't you think?"

"Very much," I agreed.

"What do the police want with him anyhow?" he said irritably. "I don't suppose they think for a minute that he had anything to do with what happened here today. If anything did happen!"

"You don't think it did?"

"I think Stewart is pretty excitable. After all, the old lady has had angina for a long time. She was due to go soon, in any event. And she was pretty feeble when I left about noon."

Then Hugo returned, and nothing more was said.

Soon after that the telephone rang in the hall, and I answered it. It was Inspector Patton.

"Miss Adams?"

"Yes, doctor."

"Nothing doing with the old man. He won't talk. But I've got an idea that he'll try to get word to somebody; he knows something, or suspects something. Or he may come back here. I rather think he will. And be on hand at eight thirty. I'm bringing Elliott up."

"Very well, doctor," I said. "I shall probably be free tomorrow."

"And again you may not, Miss Pinkerton!" he

221

said, almost blithely for him, and hung up the receiver.

We finished the meal in comparative silence. To tell the truth, it was an indifferent meal indifferently served, for the inevitable flowers had commenced to arrive, and there were long intervals while Hugo received boxes, signed for them and took them back to the pantry.

Doctor Stewart came in before we had finished, looking grave and self-important; and he waited until Hugo had left the room before he said what he had evidently come to say.

"Well, I've had the report."

"What about it?"

"It looks like poison, all right. Maybe you'll listen to me the next time, Glenn."

"What makes you think there will be a next time?"

I suspected some friction between them, but the doctor was off on the *risus sardonicus* and the other symptoms, while Hugo once more answered the doorbell. Mr. Glenn's face showed distaste, and at last he got up and flung down his napkin.

"For heaven's sake, Stewart!" he said. "I've had enough this week. I'm no medical man. Keep your knowledge for the police. They eat up that sort of thing."

Then he stalked out. He met Hugo in the hall and spoke to him briefly. Then, still irritated, he banged out of the front door. The doctor looked after him and smiled.

"Nerves!" he said. "Well, I don't know that I blame him. I'm a bit jumpy myself. And he's got a hard job ahead of him."

222

"What sort of job?" I asked.

"I happen to know that Paula Brent saw him, late this afternoon, and asked him to defend young Elliott. He has his own attorneys, but she wants him to help. He's not a criminal lawyer, but she's no fool. Glenn and his father before him have been close to the Mitchells for fifty years. It might be a shrewd move."

He left soon, and Hugo followed him out onto the porch. There they talked for a short time, and then the doctor drove away. That must have been at seven thirty.

I wondered then if that quiet talk on the veranda was the attempt to get word to somebody that the Inspector had anticipated. But the doctor's final words, which I had overheard, sounded open and reassuring enough. He had spoken from some little distance, raising his voice to do so.

"Think about it, anyhow," he said. "We don't want any more trouble, Hugo."

"You may be right, doctor."

I wandered out onto the porch myself after he had gone, and stood there for a while. The September night air was cool and bracing, and I remember taking long breaths to fill my lungs with it, and to help to clarify my mind. Think as I might, I could not put together the pieces of that puzzle. I tried to fit in Florence Lenz, but I could not. I believed that she was as capable of putting poison into the tube as any Borgia, but I could see no reason why she should. She was capable, too, of shooting Herbert Wynne; but again, why?

She was cool enough, for all her pretended fainting

223

when Charlie Elliott had bumped into her that night. She knew Herbert. She might even have learned from him that trick of shooting through a newspaper. But again, why?

I was still standing there, in the light from the front hall, when Hugo appeared from around the corner of the house and stopped near me.

"I am going out, miss," he said. "I'd be glad if you would keep an eye on my wife. She is very nervous tonight."

"I'll do that, of course."

"And—if she should decide to give you something, miss, I'll ask you to put it away carefully."

"Give me something, Hugo? What?"

"She will tell you herself. But I don't advise mentioning it to her. She might resent that. Let her bring it. If she doesn't . . ."

He made a small gesture, put on his hat and went down the drive.

I was never to see him again. It seems strange to think of that; to see again in my mind the hall light falling on his white hair and his old face, to remember him going down that drive, on his way, like Herbert, like Miss Juliet, to his death.

Was he murdered? I don't suppose we will ever know. But from the direction he took, he was on his way to Headquarters, and it is easy now to see why it was determined that he should never get there.

Sometimes I think that I had a sort of premonition that night, for I found myself shivering, and I had turned to go in when I heard Paula Brent's voice. She was standing in the shrubbery at the end of the porch, and she spoke in a low voice.

224

"Don't go in. I want to talk to you. Close that door."

"Hugo has gone out."

"I saw him. But that wife of his is still there, isn't she?"

I closed the door and moved over to her. Even in the dark I could tell that she was excited.

"Listen," she said. "There's a story going around that Miss Mitchell was poisoned. Is that true? Do you think it's true?"

"They suspect it," I said cautiously.

"Well, that lets Charlie out, doesn't it?"

"Not necessarily, Paula. But things would look better, of course."

"Tell me how it happened, and then I'll tell you something. Did that Lenz girl have anything to do with it? She was in your room, remember. And there was stuff on your tray, right under her nose."

"I haven't an idea. Yes, she could have. The question is, did she?"

And then she brought out her own news. "I've just remembered something," she said. "Although why I come to you with it I don't know! I suppose it's because I have nobody else. I can't go to my people. They think Charlie did it, and they won't talk to me. You saw the Lenz girl this morning, and the way she looked at me?"

"I did, indeed," I said briefly.

"I'd never met her before, but I knew who she was. You see, she used to be a friend of Herbert's. They were pretty close friends until he met me. Then that was over, and I guess she didn't like it much."

Well, I could imagine that Florence had not liked

it much; and I began to wonder if Paula had come that night to admit her marriage, and to say that Florence had learned about it. It turned out, however, to be something entirely different, and possibly more important.

On Monday night, as she had said before, she had met Herbert at the movies, and they went in and sat together. The theater was dark, and she had paid no attention to who sat near her. When she left, she discovered outside that she had dropped her bag, and went back for it.

It lay under her seat, and she got it and went out again. Herbert was looking at a paper, and while he did so, she examined her bag to see if her money was there. It was, but the two keys to the Mitchell house, which she always carried, had disappeared. She looked at me defiantly as she mentioned the keys, but I pretended not to notice it.

"They were gone," she said. "I had had them that evening, but they were gone."

But the point was that, while they were still standing there, the Lenz girl had come out of the theater. Herbert had not seen her. He had been rather annoyed about the keys, and he had reached into his pocket and got his own, on a key ring marked with his initials. He took one key from the ring for himself and gave her the other two. It was those keys of Herbert's which Charlie Elliott, trapped upstairs on Thursday night, had thrown out of the window.

"You are certain it was Florence?"

"Certain. I knew the other day upstairs that I had seen her somewhere, and not long ago. It just came to me tonight."

226

"And you're sure those keys were in your bag?"

"I had to be sure. I couldn't leave them at home!"

"Nobody at your house could have found them and taken them? Before you left?"

She considered that, and I thought that she was uneasy. But the next moment she dismissed the idea. Nobody there knew she had them. No, they had been stolen in the theater, and whoever took them had suspected they were there, and had slipped her bag from her knee.

"You didn't notice the people around you?"

"It was dark, of course. I didn't recognize anyone. No. But she was there. Near, too. Maybe beside me. How do I know?"

"Why don't you go to Headquarters with that?" I asked. "After all, if somebody else had keys to this house that night, and Charlie Elliott didn't, whoever it was could get in, couldn't he? Or she?"

She shook her head. "But he did," she said miserably. "He did, and they'd get that out of me. We had a quarrel that night, and he took them from me. He took my bag, with the keys in it. He knew they were there. That's why I followed him, and why I had to get the ladder. I knew he could get into the house. But if somebody else had keys, too—don't you see? They got there earlier, and that's what he says they did. He says Herbert was dead when he got into the room; that he was just dead, at that."

"Then why did he move the body?"

"He never moved the body. Where did you hear that? He heard somebody below, and he swung out the window onto the roof."

"Miss Juliet made a statement before she died,

227

Paula. She said she had seen him move the body."

"Then she lied!" she cried angrily. "She never saw that. When Charlie found him, he was in front of the bureau, with the revolver on the floor beside him, and some oil and rags on a newspaper on the dresser, as if he'd been cleaning his gun. Charlie thought it was an accident, but he didn't want to be caught there. He knew how it would look. He hid behind the chimney on the roof until the police left."

And at that minute a police car turned into the drive.

CHAPTER XXV

Among the other unrealities of that sickening night—Hugo's face with the light shining out on it, Paula and her shadowy figure and her eager voice on the end of the porch—is my recollection of that police car; of Evans getting out first, followed by Charlie Elliott, and then by the Inspector.

I can still hear Paula's gasp, and see that boy, handcuffed to Evans, standing gazing at the house; and his expression change from a sort of dogged patience to sheer joy when she rushed to him.

"Charlie! Charlie darling!"

"Sorry, honey. Only have one arm. Other's in use."

And then I can see her with her head on his shoulder, and the two police officers looking fierce and uncomfortable at the same time. They gave them their minute together, however, and let her cry her heart out, as she proceeded to do almost immediately. And Charlie Elliott tried to cheer her after his fashion.

"My turn now," he said. "Suppose you stand up and let *me* cry. Listen, dampness! How would you like to get into the car and bring me some doughnuts and a cup of decent coffee?"

But his voice was husky, and he tightened his hold on her when his humor had no effect on her.

"Now stop it," he said. "These fellows aren't as sure as they were, or why would they drag me from my warm cot and bring me to this cold, cold spot? Do you get that, sweetheart? These minions of the law are trembling in their boots right now, because they know they're off on the wrong foot. You *are* trembling, Inspector, aren't you?"

"Shaking as with a chill," said the Inspector gallantly.

Somehow this nonsense steadied her. She looked up at Charlie Elliott and smiled.

Nobody had paid the least attention to me, and now I spoke.

"You're not the only person with a chill," I said.

The Inspector saw me then, and came to me on the porch. "What about Hugo?"

"He's gone out."

He nodded. "I thought he would. I'm having him tailed. The chances are that he made for Headquarters. If he didn't, we'll soon know where he did go."

But when I told him of the talk about Mary before Hugo left, he whistled softly.

"And what might that be?" he said. "A gun? A bottle of strychnia?"

"It just might be what Miss Juliet gave her. The newspaper is my guess."

"So things are getting pretty hot, and it's time to produce the alibi!"

"That's my idea. I may be wrong."

"You're not often wrong, Miss Pinkerton!" he

230

said, and went back to his prisoner.

Then followed one of those quietly dramatic experiments which now and then a police officer with imagination will stage. Charlie Elliott was there to reproduce as faithfully as possible every move he had made in the house and on the grounds on the Monday night before. Evidently he had "come clean" to the extent of admitting that he had been there, and had agreed to duplicate his actions.

From the moment that small drama began, both the Inspector and Evans were absorbed in it. I doubt if they even know that Paula and I were following. Now and then the Inspector asked a question, but much of it took place in silence, save for the boy's own explanations as they went along.

He led first to the street, and turned from there into the next property. "I got out of the taxi at the corner," he said, "and turned in here."

He went back perhaps a hundred yards and stopped there. The house was not much more than a shadow from there, and he stopped and surveyed it.

"I'd been here before," he said. "I'd followed Paula one night. The side door is over there."

After that he moved through the shrubbery, still leading Evans by that handcuff, and partway across the lawn he stopped again.

"This is where I was when I saw somebody coming out of the side door. I've told you that. You can see how dark it is, and why I couldn't tell whether it was a man or a woman."

"And they went toward the rear of the house?"

"Yes."

The Inspector was still standing, gazing toward

the side door. "Listen, Elliott," he said. "You must have thought something about that figure. After all, why should anybody slip out of that door at that hour of the night? You must have thought a lot about it, if your story's the right one."

I thought young Elliott hesitated. "I tell you," he replied, "I have thought about it. I haven't thought of much else. Remember, I didn't see who it was. But at the time I sort of took it for granted that it was either Hugo or Doctor Stewart. I knew the old lady had a bad heart; everybody knew it."

"But you couldn't see the doctor going toward the kitchen. Is that it?"

"Well, hardly that. His car wasn't in sight, and he might have cut across lots from another case nearby. There are no fences. No, it isn't that. Why would he shoot Wynne? What would be the idea? That's where I bring up every time."

"All right. Let that ride. What then?"

"Just what I've told you."

We moved toward the house, and at the side entrance he stopped.

"This part was easy. I'd got Paula's keys, as I've explained, and I had no trouble with this door; but I was pretty well lost when I got to the top of the back stairs. I could hear Hugo snoring, however, in the back room, so I tried the other key on the door there. I had lighted a match to do that, and I found myself on the landing of the second floor."

We went on up, and he repeated what he had done. Apparently Mary was still in the kitchen, and unsuspicious. In the hall on the second floor Charlie Elliott stopped and smiled faintly.

"I stopped here," he said. "I'd been blind crazy up to that minute, but the job began to look too much like housebreaking about that time. I don't mind saying that up to this point, I might have killed him if I'd had a gun. After that I began to feel pretty much like a damned fool."

But the light had been burning overhead, and so he had kept on.

Halfway up to the third floor, or a little more, he stopped again.

"If somebody will go ahead, and turn on that light, it will help," he said. "I was here when I saw him first."

The Inspector went on up, and we stood there waiting. In the semidarkness I saw Charlie reach down his free hand and grope for Paula's; and so they waited, those two children, until the light went on.

"I was here," he said. "I stopped and looked across into the room; and at first I thought he was looking for something under the bureau. But his position was queer, and when he didn't move, I saw that something was wrong. I nearly turned and ran then! But of course I couldn't. Whether he was sick or hurt or just blind drunk, I had to go on. And I did."

Up in the room itself he repeated what he had done. He had stooped over the body, but had not moved it. He saw the wound, and knew at once that Herbert was dead.

"How long dead?" said the Inspector. "Was he still warm? Was he limber?"

"I don't know. Or was that a trap? I didn't touch him, I tell you. I thought at first of lifting him onto the bed. Then I remembered not to touch anything.

233

First order of all good policemen."

"But you went over and looked at the bed?"

"I don't think so. I was still stooping when I heard somebody on the stairs, and I had to get out. I knew of the roof, and I can show you how I did it, if you like."

"And have to get off with a ladder again? Not on your life! And how do I know you haven't got a ladder there now, my lad?"

Well, that was meant as a joke, and so we received it. Any relief in that grisly business was welcome. But the Inspector was sober and businesslike enough immediately.

"How long had you stood in that shrubbery?"

"Only long enough to get my bearings."

"And you heard no shot?"

"I may have. I wouldn't have paid any attention. Too many backfires these days."

"You didn't connect what you found with the figure you'd seen?"

He hesitated. "I'd rather not answer that."

"Go on, Charlie. Tell them," said Paula unexpectedly.

"How did I know that it wasn't Paula?" he said slowly. "I know now that it couldn't have been, but you see what I mean. I didn't know then that they were married, but I did know she couldn't see him at her home, and that she came here."

"You'd just left her, hadn't you?"

"He had to look for a taxi," Paula said bravely. "I could have got here before he did, and he knew that. I didn't, but that's what he thought."

"You had her keys, didn't you?"

"She could have whistled, or something. I'd better

234

explain what I mean. I didn't think she'd killed him. You understand that. I didn't think anyone had killed him. But if she had told him something . . ."

"That I cared for you, and not for him," Paula put in bravely.

"Well, you see what that would mean. I just didn't want her mixed up with it. That's all. And of course I wasn't sure that it was Paula." He glanced at her. "Sorry, Paula, but you know it, too. Wynne always had a girl or two on the string. He was that sort."

The Inspector flicked a glance at me. "All right," he said. "Now we'll go over the ladder business. I'll need you for that, Miss Brent."

But they never did go over the ladder business. When they had reached the front door, passing solemnly by that room where Miss Juliet lay in state, surrounded by her flowers, it was to find an officer in the lower hall, with a message for the Inspector.

He turned to me with a grave face. "Break this to Mary as gently as you can," he said. "The old man was knocked down by a hit-and-run driver not very far from the house, and died on his way to the hospital."

CHAPTER XXVI

That night remains to me one of the most horrible in my experience.

It was necessary to break the news to Mary, and she went into utter and complete collapse. Hugo's body was still in the hospital mortuary, and it was useless to ask her what her wishes were with regard to it. By ten o'clock I had got the doctor, and he gave her something to keep her quiet; but when he had gone, I found myself virtually alone.

A dim light burned in Miss Juliet's room, and the entire house was redolent with the sickly odor of funeral flowers. I had opened the door on the landing, so that I could go back now and then to see Mary, and I sat in the room which had been mine, and which adjoined the large front room where Miss Juliet lay in state.

I was very tired. It was Friday night, and the amount of real sleep I had had since the Monday before was negligible. But as usual in such cases, I was too weary to sleep. I threw myself, still in my uniform, on my bed; but once down, my mind began to fill with clues, conjectures, what not.

237

Once more I tried to reconstruct what had happened in that upper room on Monday night, but with the same lack of success. I could see Herbert, entering by the front door, and cheerfully enough. He would still have the *Eagle* in his pocket, at least probably. And I could see him in his room later on, preparing to undress, taking out his revolver first, and laying it and then the newspaper on the bureau. I could even see someone entering that room, but it would not have been Charlie Elliott, or Herbert would not have remained in that chair. He would have leaped to his feet, surely; have sensed trouble, even reached for his revolver.

But he had not gotten up. He had looked up, perhaps, from untying his shoe. He had almost certainly not been alarmed at all, although he may have been surprised. But he had stayed in his chair, perhaps for some time. There had been conversation of some sort, with the killer getting out his handkerchief under some pretense or other, or keeping on his gloves, and edging toward that revolver on the dresser. But Herbert had not expected to be killed. He had looked up, and had got a bullet in his forehead, perhaps even before he sensed that there was any danger.

I could go as far as that, but no further. I believed Paula's story, and Charlie Elliott's. I believe that Herbert had been dead when Charlie Elliott entered that room. But nothing in all of this explained how the *Eagle* had become the *News,* or why that scrap of paper had had powder marks on it, or had been a week old. Nor did any of it bear any relationship to a plot about life insurance.

238

I went over Miss Juliet's statement in my mind. Perhaps young Elliott had moved to the bed; he was excited. Perhaps she had seen him coming forward as she said, and then stooping over the body. But she had said that he had moved it, dragged it across the floor! Had she seen that, or had she imagined it later?"

I was roused at eleven by the doorbell, and I went wearily down the stairs. It seemed to me that I had made a million excursions up and down those stairs; that I had worn hollows in them with my feet. I had expected a reporter, but it was the Inspector himself, looking even more grave than the circumstances seemed to warrant.

He stepped into the hall, and closed the door behind him. "Look here," he said, " have you your automatic?"

"You told me not to bring it."

"Well, I've brought you one," he said, and laid it on the table beside me. "Just remember to take off the safety before you snap it at anybody."

"I don't want it," I said. "I don't want it. I want to go home and go to sleep forever."

"You'll take a good chance of going to sleep forever if you don't keep a gun handy in this house," he retorted grimly. "I'm not trying to scare you, but I put you on this job and I'm responsible for you. I'm not sending you after Hugo."

"After Hugo?"

"I think Hugo was murdered, deliberately run down and killed as he crossed the street by the Manchester place. Our man saw it done, but he had only a glimpse of the car."

239

"He was murdered!"

"He's dead, anyhow."

He looked at me, and I must have been pale, for he put a hand on my shoulder. "You're a brave young woman, Miss Pinkerton," he said, "and you're not going to quit on us now. Nor are we going to quit on you. Just remember that. And now I'm going up and talk to Mary."

He was closeted with her for some time, and after that I heard him moving about the rear of the house. He stopped at the washstand in the hall to wash his hands, and he was drying them when he came back to me, in the library.

He put me into a comfortable chair before he said anything.

"Just lean back and listen," he said. "I think I've got this thing doped out, and I've made some plans to close it up. But I can tell you a certain amount. Here was what at first looked like a suicide, but with no contact marks. There were two possibilities. This boy had a fortune in insurance, and he knew that the old lady was desperate for money. It might, of course, have been accidental death, but Herbert wasn't cleaning his gun when it happened. He'd done it earlier that evening, between eight and nine. And if the bullet mark on the fireplace and other signs meant anything, he had been in a chair when it happened, taking off his shoes.

"Still, there are ways of committing suicide so that it looks like something else, and that newspaper would probably have thrown us off the scent entirely, if I had happened to open it. As a matter of fact, I picked it up and looked at it, but as you know, the

240

front and back pages were whole; no bullet marks on them. It wasn't until you found that scrap here in the library and gave it to me that I began to veer toward the suicide idea. But even there I was puzzled. The scrap was from a paper a week old, and by all the evidence it should have been from the *Eagle*. It wasn't. I put our fellows on it, and it was from the *News*.

"That might mean a lot, or it might not. I can tell you now that I got that newspaper from Mary just now. She'd had it hidden from Hugo all week, but she told me a little while ago where to find it."

He took it from his pocket and gave it to me. It was much as he had described such a paper, that day in the office. Closed, it was whole; opened, it showed part of a bullet hole, and certain powder marks and scorchings. One corner was missing and the Inspector took out the scrap from his wallet and fitted it into place.

"Now we have to think of this," he went on. "Miss Juliet confessed to a certain amount, but not all she knew. She had seen that newspaper, and Mary admits that she knew from Herbert how such a trick could be pulled. She got that newspaper that night and gave it to Mary to hide. Hugo was not to know about it, or anybody.

"What I figure is that she lay in her bed that night, and she suddenly remembered that newspaper on the bureau, and had her moment of temptation. Mary may have told her that night that there was considerable insurance. Mary had a way of learning things she was not supposed to know. You can see Miss Juliet's argument. After all, she was poor and

241

insurance companies are rich. And she couldn't bring that boy back to life."

"I don't believe it. I don't believe she would lend herself to a thing like that. To profit by her own nephew's death . . . !"

"Nevertheless, that is what she did. And that's our scrap of paper."

"And he killed himself after all!"

"Who said he killed himself? All I'm saying is that whatever opinion she formed later, that night she believed that he had killed himself. It wasn't until we began working on the case that she began to doubt it. She had seen young Elliott escaping, but she knew him. It wouldn't occur to her that a boy she knew would kill. You know the idea; she'd known his people. He'd been engaged to Paula. An accident, or a suicide, but not murder. Not then, anyhow."

"She came to murder, just the same," I said with some bitterness.

"Surely she did. So did you. So did I. But let's get on with this. I have to go." He looked at his watch.

"Now take the other side. Here's a clear case of murder against Charlie Elliott; so clear that the District Attorney is going to have to be restrained if anything happens to it. Young Elliott was jealous. More than that, he was frantic. He had followed the girl, and he knew she was coming to this house at night. Pretty hard to swallow, all that, for Herbert Wynne was no good and he knew it.

"Now, it's at least conceivable that, leaving out the matter of the insurance, young Elliott might kill Wynne. Here's the girl's story about Wynne being followed, and having to carry a revolver. It all fits.

But there are one or two things left over; this newspaper, for one thing. It's hardly conceivable that Elliott fired at Wynne through that paper. But if he did, for any reason, why was the paper a week old?"

"You mean, it had been prepared in advance?"

"Good for you. That's just what I do mean. You said something that day in the office, when you said that a murder could be made to look like a suicide. The only answer to this newspaper is that this murder was to look like an accident, and that if trouble came there was the alibi—the paper. Only one thing slipped up. Mary got that paper and hid it. She hid it, if you want to know, in a mason jar and set it into a crock of apple butter in the cellar!"

I gazed at him with eyes that must have been sunk deep in my head. "Then it was Hugo, after all?"

"It was not Hugo. I only know this; that if some plans I've laid work out as I expect them to, I ought to be able to tell you in the morning. Or sooner!"

And with that he went away. Even now, looking back, I find it hard to forgive him for that. He might have told me something, have given me some hint. He could trust me; I had worked hard for him. But he did not even tell me how he had planned to protect me.

I think he had his own moment of doubt as he went away, for he stood in the hall and looked at me, and then at the stairs behind me.

"Good night," he said. "Don't do too much running about; and take the gun upstairs with you." Then he went away, and as I locked and bolted the door behind him, I again had that curious little shiver of fear.

The house was certainly eerie that night. It creaked
and rapped incessantly, and over it all hung the
heavy funereal odor of those flowers in the front
room. The hall was filled with it, and it had even
penetrated back to Mary's room.

I had taken the gun upstairs with me, but I don't
mind saying that after a time I began to feel that no
revolver would be of any use against the phantoms
with which my mind insisted on filling those old
rooms; with Miss Juliet and Herbert, and now with
Hugo. Only Mary left, out of that family of ghosts,
and she sleeping the sleep of drugs and exhaustion in
that back room.

At half past twelve I went back to look at her, but
she was quiet. Even seeing her, at least alive and
substantial, calmed me somewhat; and I was quiet
and somewhat comforted when I left her. Somewhat
comforted! That is even funny now. For it was that
visit to Mary which precipitated my own catastro-
phe.

Her cat was lying on her bed, and I picked the
animal up to carry it into the front hall. Perhaps it is
a superstition, but I do not like cats around where
there are dead, and it was my intention to put it out.

On the landing, however, it escaped and ran up the
third-floor stairs. I disliked intensely the idea of
following it, but at last I decided to, turning on the
hall light first, and then going on up, calling it as I
went.

"Here, Tom!" I called. "Come here! Tom! Tom!"

The sound of my own voice in that quiet house
sounded cavernous, and I was not happy to catch a
glimpse of the animal, and going into Herbert's

244

room at that. But I had started, and I meant to see the thing through. So I followed him in.

There was a faint light in the room from the hall below, and by it I worked my way toward the dresser and the bracket light beside it. I could see it, faintly gleaming; and then suddenly I could not see at all. Very quietly the door had closed behind me!

I was paralyzed with terror. I stood perfectly still, my arm upraised toward the bracket, and now I was certain that there was someone in the room. Yet nothing moved. There were only the usual creaks and groans of the old house, swaying in the September breeze. Then, I was certain that the creaks were approaching me. I had my back to the room, but I could hear them, coming closer; and just as I opened my mouth to scream, I felt hands close on my throat. I was being slowly strangled from behind.

CHAPTER XXVII

Whoever it was, those hands were prodigiously strong. I was utterly helpless. Sometimes, even now, I waken at night, dripping with a hot sweat, again feeling that terrible struggle for breath, and once more trying to loosen those deadly fingers.

I was incredulous at first, I know. This thing could not be happening to me. It was not possible that someone was trying to kill me. Then I knew that it was possible, and that I was about to die. I can remember that, and I can remember when I began to lose consciousness. My knees went first; I could not stand. I was sagging, falling. Then I must have gone entirely, although I have no memory of that.

I came to myself very slowly. It was difficult to breathe. My throat was swollen and I could not turn my head. And the air, when I did get it, seemed to do me no good. My lungs labored; I could hear myself gasping.

I tried to move, although my head was bursting. But I could not move. I seemed to be in a half-sitting position, in a narrow space, and as I became more conscious, I put out my hand. I touched a wall, and in another direction, only a couple of feet away, I

247

touched another wall. It was some time, in my dazed condition, before I realized that one of these walls was a door, and a still longer time before the facts began to dawn on me; that I was locked in the closet of Herbert's room, and that the air supply was very bad.

So completely was I engrossed with my own position and with that struggle for air, which was partially due to the œdema of my throat, that it must have been several minutes before I so much as attempted to orient myself. It was even longer before I became aware of the complete and utter silence in the house. Then I tried to call out, but I could only make a hoarse and guttural noise which could not have been heard beyond the door of the room, so I gave that up. It took air which, apparently, I could not spare.

The closet was stiflingly hot, and my legs began to cramp. I tried to stand up, but I was too weak to rise. My mind was clearer, however.

I tried hammering on the door, but the really dreadful silence continued. And then, far away, I heard a sound. It might have been anything, but it began to sound like someone climbing the stairs. And that, I realized very soon, was what it was. Whoever it was came very slowly, and seemed now and then to stop; but that inevitable progress continued. The stairs creaked, the railing groaned, as if someone was holding on to it. Suddenly it occurred to me that it was the murderer coming back, and I had an attack of panic so terrible that, even as I write this, I find myself in a hot sweat of fear.

The footsteps reached the third floor at last, still with that curious wavering advance, and the unknown seemed to stand in the doorway for some time, like a runner who has finished a race. Then they came into the room and stopped there. I could hear a sort of gasping for breath, and then there followed another stealthy movement; a movement toward the closet door and, after what seemed like a moment of listening, the turning of the key in that door.

Even now I wonder about that. Was there a sort of late repentance for it? A final decision to give me a chance for life before I smothered? I cannot believe it. But I do know that with the turning of the key I tried to scream, and that my vocal cords would not respond.

Something else did, however. Just what strength I received at the instant I do not know. I have a vague sort of recollection of suddenly being able to stand, and of being stronger that I had ever been before. I recall that, and that as the key turned I pushed against the door with a frenzy born of desperation. It flew open, and it evidently struck whoever stood outside, and struck hard; for I heard a grunt in the darkness and then a heavy fall and silence. I actually fell over that inert figure as I rushed out, and the next instant I was flying down the stairs, and almost straight into the barrel of a revolver held by Inspector Patton.

"In Herbert's room," I croaked. "Quick! In Herbert's room."

Then, almost on the spot where poor Hugo had collapsed that very day, I fainted again.

When I came to, I was lying on my bed in my own small room adjoining Miss Juliet's. The Inspector was standing beside the bed, and there was a sound of shuffling feet outside. The Inspector frowned and hastily closed the door into the hall, but I knew only too well what that shuffling meant: the careful carrying of a stretcher, where men do not keep step, but walk with a broken rhythm to avoid the swinging which might jar whoever lies on it. When the Inspector came back to the bed, I was looking at him, he has said since, and making strange noises in my throat.

"Don't try to talk. How do you feel? All right?"

I nodded. "Ice," I croaked. "Ice on my throat. Swollen."

I realized then that there was a policeman just outside the door, for the Inspector sent him for some cracked ice in a towel, and then looked at me gravely.

"I'll have to be running along," he said. "But I can't go without saying that I owe you a number of things, including one of the profoundest apologies of my life; and a policeman's life is full of them! I told you once that down at Headquarters we had a lot of wall-eyed pikes who called themselves detectives. Well, I'm the king piker of the lot. All I can do is to thank God it's no worse, little Miss Pinkerton."

"Who was it?" I croaked. My lips were still swollen, and my tongue felt thick in my mouth. When he said later that I was hissing like a teakettle with excitement, he was pretty nearly right.

And, of course, the policeman chose that moment to come running with a piece of ice as big as his head, and on top of that I heard the telephone ringing wildly downstairs. Somebody below answered it and called up.

"You're wanted, Inspector. Fellow seems to be in a hurry."

"Who is it?"

"Name's Henderson, he says."

250

The Inspector flung out of the room, and I could hear him running down the stairs. I got off the bed, and went as far as the landing, feeling weak, my knees shaking. When I had got a firm grip on the stair rail and looked over, it was to see the Inspector at the telephone, a tall lank figure in a gray suit; the front doors wide open and men standing on the porch, and beyond them again, something shining and black; the police ambulance.

The Inspector was barking into the telephone.

"What's the matter, Henderson?"

He listened for a minute.

"How long ago?" he shouted. . . . "An hour or more? Good God, man! Get over there and break a window. I'll be right along."

He gave a few orders, and then, seeing me on the stairs, he called to me.

"How are you now? Strong enough to take a ride? You won't have to talk!"

I nodded, and was about to turn back for a coat when he called again.

"If you're coming, come now. We've got no time to spare."

With that he shot out of the front door and down the steps. I followed him as best I could, and I was barely in the car, and had not managed to close the door, before he had let in the clutch and we were on our way. Never before have I traveled at such a rate, and I hope never to do so again. A motorcycle policeman had materialized from nowhere, and he preceded us, keeping his siren going, and clearing the way. We dashed through traffic lights and past pedestrians, having only a glimpse of their astonished faces, and in all that time he spoke only once.

"It's Paula Brent," he said, not looking at me. "She's in the garage; locked in, according to Henderson. And he can't make her hear him."

To my surprise I found that I could speak, although huskily.

"Locked in! She hasn't tried to kill herself?"

"I rather think," he said slowly, "that someone has tried to do that for her. And we can thank little Henderson if it wasn't successful. I don't even know that yet."

"How?"

"Carbon-monoxide gas, apparently. But it is a large garage. There's just a chance . . ."

His voice trailed off, and at that moment we turned into the alley behind the Brent house.

There was no trouble in finding what we were looking for. Halfway along the block was a private garage, brightly lighted, and inside of it a small group of people bending over something on the floor which I could not see. Even before we had got out of the car, a figure detached itself from the group, and I saw that it was Mr. Henderson.

"We've sent for the ambulance, Inspector. It ought to be here any minute."

"Then she's living?"

"Yes."

"Thank God! Who is in there?"

"Her father and mother, and my wife. Our roundsman, too, but he has just come. It was my wife who sent for the ambulance."

And I seemed to feel his pride in that, even as I climbed out of the car and went into the garage.

Paula Brent was lying on the cement floor, very still and barely breathing.

CHAPTER XXVIII

She lay at the rear of her own small coupé, and as the group about her moved back, I examined her, but I had had little experience of carbon-monoxide cases, and I was rather at a loss. I suggested artificial respiration until the ambulance arrived; and it was the motorcycle man who gave it. I myself was still too weak.

I found the Inspector bending over me as I stooped. "Any marks on her? Has she been hurt?"

"I'm not sure. There is a lump on the back of her head, but she may have fallen."

He left the group and I saw him prowling about the garage, but apparently he found nothing, and I think he expected to find nothing. There was glass on the floor under the window, where Mr. Henderson had broken his way in, but that was all. I saw him talking to Mr. Henderson, and soon after that he took a pocket flashlight and went out into the alley. When he came back, with little Henderson trotting at his heels, he was carrying a small key in his handkerchief, and he wrapped it carefully and put it in his pocket.

If I had had any doubt that an attempt had been made that night to murder Paula Brent, it died then. She had been locked in that garage, and left to die.

The ambulance arrived very soon after that, and we followed it to the hospital. A queer-looking object I must have been, at that. I had worked at St. Luke's, and the night porter knew me well.

"Looks as though you'd been in some sort of mix-up, Miss Adams," he said.

"Mix-up is the word, John," I said, "and if there is anyone still in the kitchen, I'd like to have some strong black coffee."

He promised to send it to me, and I followed the Inspector to the Emergency Ward. There were five or six people around the table there, and they had sent for the pulmotor. What with a couple of internes, the night supervisor and what not, I could get only a glimpse of Paula, lying there still and rather childish. Then the group closed in, and somebody brought me my coffee.

They worked over her most of what was left of the night, and it was gray dawn before she was out of danger. The Inspector had disappeared as soon as she began to improve, but he returned again shortly after daylight, to pace the hospital corridor until he was allowed to see her. When that time came, he cleared the room, except for me, and then drawing up a chair beside the bed proceeded to question her; rather gently, as one might interrogate a child.

But she knew very little. After that experiment at the Mitchell house she had meant to go home, as the Inspector had ordered. She was happy and excited, however, for she felt certain that the police meant to

254

release Charlie Elliott. She had told the Inspector, too, about Florence and the keys, and all in all she was very hopeful.

So she did not got home. She drove about until half past eleven or so. Then she went home and put her car in the garage. She had cut off her engine when she heard someone walking in the alley. That did not disturb her, and she was on her way to close the garage doors when she saw a man entering. There was a light in the alley, and her first alarm came when she saw that he had something dark tied over the lower part of his face.

That frightened her, and she turned to escape by the small door leading to the house. It must have been then that he struck her down, for she remembered no more until she awakened in the hospital.

That was all she knew, and it was Mr. Henderson, still waiting below, who supplied some of the gaps in her story.

Apparently it was as Inspector Patton had said the day before, that the arrest of Charlie Elliott, and his own part in it, was the nearest to drama that his life had ever touched. However that may be, apparently from the time on Monday night when he had heard Paula and Charlie quarreling in the alley, he had taken an avid interest in their affairs.

On that Friday night, then, he had heard Paula taking out her car about eight, and when she was not back by ten or thereabouts, he grew a little anxious.

"I've got no children," he explained, "so I've always been fond of Paula. And of Charlie Elliott, too," he hastened to add.

By eleven, when she still had not returned, he

spoke to his wife. She, however, was not as fond of Paula as he was, and she told him to go to bed and quit worrying about a girl young enough to be his daughter. He said nothing more to her and he did go to bed; but he lay awake and listened, and around eleven thirty or maybe a quarter to twelve, she drove in and cut off her engine, and soon after, he heard the garage doors close.

He turned over then to go to sleep, but after five minutes or so he heard the engine going again. He got up and looked out. The garage across the alley was dark, but there was no question about the motor. It was going, and going hard. He would have gone over then, but his wife was indignant by that time, and so he had crawled back into bed.

"You'd think that child didn't know anything about a car," she told him. "If she wants to try out her engine, let her do it."

"But there's no light in the place."

"How do you know that? She's probably using a hand flash. Now go to sleep."

He did not go to sleep, however, and it was perhaps a quarter to one when his wife at last seemed settled for the night. All that time he had heard the motor running, but at that time or thereabouts he heard the engine stop, and he went to the window again. He was worried, for some reason or other. He went to the window, he said, so that when Paula left the garage by the small door, he could see her and then settle down. There was a light on at the Brent place, and he could always see anyone who left the garage at night and went toward the house.

But she did not leave the garage. He waited for

256

perhaps fifteen minutes, and then he resolutely put on his clothes and went carefully down the stairs and out of the house. He felt, I gathered, rather foolish, and he did not want his wife to waken and find him gone.

"You know how women are," he said to the Inspector, as if that explained it.

He found the Brent garage doors locked, both the double ones on the alley and the small one toward the house, and the garage itself dark and quiet. He began to feel foolish, but that odd sense of something wrong still persisted and at last he went back to the house and got his flashlight.

His wife wakened as he fumbled for it, and he made an excuse of hearing a noise downstairs, and said something about burglars. It was the wrong thing, evidently, for she tried to keep him from going down at all; and at last he simply went, asserting himself in a fashion that still evidently startled him. He mopped his face as he told it.

But he took the flash and went across the alley and around to a side window, and he was sure that he could see Paula lying on the cement floor, behind the car. It was then that he went back and telephoned, first to Headquarters and then to the Mitchell house.

As to the stopping of the engine at a quarter before one, he believed what later proved to be the fact—that it had stopped because the gas tank was empty.

Most of all that I only learned later, of course. I was still with Paula when the Inspector came back and again began to question her. She was much better by that time, although she was still very white.

"Can you tell me what you did yesterday, Paula?"

257

he asked. "Go through the day, as briefly as you can."

Well, her day had been fairly full, all things considered.

It began with my telephone message, and her mistake in the hour. She had reached the house at ten, had been too late to see Miss Juliet, and had asked me to take her into the house.

"I know all that. I found that certificate, Paula. It's safe."

She colored faintly, but went on. She had met Florence Lenz in my room, and learned who she was. Florence had been rude to her. She had had trouble in getting out of the house, but had managed it, and gone home to lunch. Early in the afternoon a woman named Henderson, a terrible person apparently, who browbeat her nice little husband, had telephoned that Miss Juliet was dead. She was the sort who could not wait to pass on bad news, and Paula resented her tone. She had simply hung up the receiver.

But she was frightened just the same. If Miss Juliet's statement was damaging to Charlie Elliott, there would be no way of disproving it now. It was not until later in the afternoon, when Doctor Stewart came in to see her mother, that she learned the possibility of poison.

"But if it was poison, doctor," she had said, "wouldn't that exonerate Charlie? They couldn't blame him for that."

The two of them were alone in the library by that time, and she made up her mind to tell the doctor at least a part of the story. She had done that, and while she did so, something had occurred to her for the first time. If she was married to Herbert, she was entitled

258

to that insurance money. And if she had that money, she could afford to employ a lawyer.

When the doctor left, she had telephoned to Arthur Glenn, but he was still in court. She went to his office, however, and waited for him until he came in at something after four. She had thought of him, because he had been Miss Juliet's lawyer, and his father had represented the Mitchell family before him. If he worked with Charlie's attorneys, it would show that he really believed him innocent.

But sitting there waiting, with Florence busily typing in another room, she had had time to look at her. And it was then that she had remembered where she had seen Florence before; coming out of that moving-picture theater on Monday night, and giving her a cold stare as she passed.

CHAPTER XXIX

Strange as it seems now, in all the strain of that night and the frenzied endeavors to save Paula Brent, I had given little or no thought to my own experience. And now, in that hospital room, all I craved was sleep. Curiosity was dead in me. I found my head drooping while she talked, and when, later on, the Inspector bundled me in his car and drove me home, he tells me that I slept all the way.

But we did not leave immediately when Paula had finished. Instead the Inspector got up and, opening the door to the hall, beckoned to someone. The next moment Charlie Elliott was in the room and bending over Paula's bed.

"Darling!" he said thickly. "You poor darling."

"Somebody gave me the rap, Charlie!"

"I know about that."

But if I had expected any emotional scene between them that morning, I did not get it. True, they had a tight grip on each other, as though they meant never to let go. But these modern youngsters camouflage what they feel, so what she said was, "You need a shave, you know. What did you do? Break

261

out with dynamite?"

He glanced at the Inspector, benignly watching them.

"Those bozos down at the jail said that after almost a week they'd be glad to pay me to get out."

"I don't blame them! I suppose you tried to be funny."

"*Be* funny!" he protested. "I *was* funny. Ask the Inspector; *he* knows. Tell her that joke of mine about the Marines and the cow, Inspector.

But it was camouflage, and the next minute he grinned at us, and waved toward the door.

"We're about six months behind in our necking," he observed, "and I'm old-fashioned about necking. I don't like an audience."

When I glanced back through the open door a minute later, he was on his knees beside Paula's bed, with an arm thrown over her. And she was crying.

I was almost beyond noticing, however. Somehow the Inspector got me down to his car, and as I have said, I slept all the way home. I remember getting out of the car and climbing the stairs to my sitting room. I have a faint recollection of Dick hopping about wildly, and then I was on my couch and I did not waken until the stealthy clatter of dishes roused me. I looked up, and Mrs. Merwin was carrying in a tray for two.

"Here's some breakfast, dearie," she said cheerfully. "And some for the gentleman. . . . You look a wreck. It must have been a bad case," she added, appraising me carefully. Then she left.

I began to laugh. I laughed until I found the Inspector holding a cup of coffee under my nose and sternly telling me to drink it and quit it.

"Quit it!" I said hysterically. "I have quit. I'm through. Washed up."

He paid absolutely no attention to that, and while I sipped my coffee, he went over and talked to the canary.

"Well, Dick," he said, "your mistress is in a bad humor, and there will be no sugar for either of us for a while. I don't know that I blame her, either. And we have to remember that. But outside of the temper, she's rather a dear person, and I'm fond of her. In fact, I'm very fond of her."

"Stop talking nonsense," I said sharply. "And tell me about last night."

"It's a long story. I need food first."

"If that gun you gave me wasn't in the jardinière . . ."

"In the jardinière!" he said. "My God!"

And then, between mouthfuls of a hearty breakfast, he began his story.

"As a matter of record," he said, "I owe a part of the solution of these two crimes—or maybe three—to you. You did a good piece of work without knowing it, when you marooned those two poor devils on the roof yesterday. And I repaid you by getting you damned near choked to death! You can consider last night's apology repeated, and then some. But I have an excuse, such as it is. We were there all right, outside the house. But we were watching the doors. We knew that this person we were after had keys to that side door and, by all the laws of probability, would use them.

"What we did not know was that a window would

263

be unlocked and subsequently used.

"When we found that open window, it was too late.

"But let's get at this in orderly fashion. I'll say this. Up to between four o'clock and five yesterday afternoon you knew almost as much as I did. You knew about the insurance, and that Herbert Wynne hadn't carried out the plan as he was supposed to. You'd seen Miss Juliet's confession, and you knew that it definitely implicated Charlie Elliott. And you knew, too, that she had been murdered in her turn.

"Charlie Elliott couldn't have done that. And as you said yesterday after you read that statement of hers—or did I say it?—that statement left out certain facts which were important. What about that newspaper? Why had she left that out of her statement? That set me to thinking.

"Now, what sort of woman was Miss Juliet Mitchell? She was honest, wasn't she? And all week she has been lying in her bed and worrying about the thing she had done. At last she decides to make a statement, telling about what she found in that room that night; that is all she had to tell, but she was determined to tell it. Yet after Mary produced that paper last night, I knew what I had already suspected: that Miss Juliet hadn't told all she knew. She never mentioned that paper. Why?

"But let's forget Monday for a minute, and get on to yesterday. She was poisoned. I was pretty sure of that when I found that tablet on the ground, and our fellows confirm it. But I'm here to say, hard as it sounds, that if her murderer had left well enough alone, I believe that Charlie Elliott would have gone to the chair.

"She was feeble. She had this heart trouble. And I doubt if she'd have lived until the trial came up.

"Here the peculiar psychology of any intelligent killer comes to our aid. No killer is content to let well enough alone. That's probably why they return to the scenes of their crimes. And this killer of ours was in a bad way; lying awake at night wondering if he had covered his tracks. Thinking of this, afraid of that. God knows whether there's a hell or not, but the killer doesn't need one. He lives it on earth.

"And remember, Miss Juliet hadn't mentioned that newspaper in her statement.

"Let's go back over that original scheme. I'm inclined to think that Herbert originated the idea. I know this much: he was to get five thousand down, and another five when he had drowned himself, or pretended to.

"The scheme was, of course, to get away from here, and to make a new start. The Lenz girl was to go with him, and as far as I know, it may have been her idea."

"It's the sort of thing she would think of," I agreed.

"Now that's all very pretty. You can see Hugo falling for it. But I have an idea that the original amount was not to be so large; enough to pay Herbert what he was to get, pay Miss Juliet's debts, and leave enough for the servants' legacies. One of the things which looked odd was Hugo's astonishment when he learned that a hundred thousand dollars was involved. I believe he was frightened, from that time on.

"Much of the insurance plot I knew or suspected; but it was only yesterday that I learned that the Lenz girl had been Herbert's lady love until he met Paula, early last spring. The plot had preceded that. That brought Florence Lenz in in some way, but I couldn't see how. And there were other things to be worked out. I'd been over that upper room, but without conviction, as you know. So there was the explanation of those night invasions of the Mitchell house, and finding Charlie Elliott back there on Thursday.

"Then there was the searching of Herbert's clothes by Mary and Miss Juliet, and I suppose by Hugo before that. I knew it had been done, but why? Hugo I can understand. Paula had said that Herbert had threatened to leave a letter somewhere, so that, if anything happened to him, she could produce it. He was after that letter. But what were Mary and the old lady looking for?

"That's fairly easy. I think Miss Juliet believed that he had killed himself, and there's a convention about such affairs. At least she believed that there was. All suicides left letters, she believed, and where was Herbert's?

"You get that, of course? All right. Now, she has gone as far as she can, and she is miserable. She has saved the Mitchell house and the Mitchell honor; but she is a sinning woman, and she will have to meet her God before long. She can't stand it. She tells Hugo she is going to confess, she tells Arthur Glenn. And then she doesn't confess after all!

"It wouldn't work, so far as I was concerned, and I began to go back over that poisoning. Why did she have to go? She had done her part. And then, sometime between four and five that afternoon, those two boys you'd held on the roof came in to give me something, and I began to see daylight."

He paused, and poured out another cup of coffee; it was cold by that time.

"Now go over the people involved in this case. Hugo didn't smoke at all. Herbert smoked cigarettes incessantly. There were only two men connected with it at all who smoked cigars. And what those boys had found was an almost entire cigar of a good brand. You have to remember that the press has known almost as much of this case as I have. The D. A. has seen to that." He smiled wryly. "Also a good many of the newspapermen, especially the younger ones, never had believed that Charlie Elliott was guilty. And Elliott was a cigarette smoker.

"But I had to be sure. I had to be sure that Evans hadn't smoked a cigar there the night I got him out on the roof. Well, he had, but it was a stogie, and he still had it in his mouth when he got down the ladder.

"This cigar was under some leaves in the gutter, and we'd overlooked it. But one of these reporters, a fellow named Davidson, crawled out there to see what I was doing below when I threw that ladder away, and he uncovered it. I took it to the laboratory, and while a lot of this Sherlock Holmes stuff about tobacco ashes and so on is only good for fiction, they did think it had been out in the weather three or four days. They didn't know when or how I got it. That was the opinion, anyhow.

"That gave me something. I could imagine that a part of the camouflage in that room which fooled Herbert Wynne on Monday night, and maybe let this unknown get hold of that revolver, was the lighting of that cigar. It hadn't been smoked more than a couple of minutes.

"Well, who smoked cigars on this case? Only two men, and you know who they are."

"Mr. Glenn and the doctor!"

"Precisely. And the whole case came down to which of them profited by Miss Juliet's death. By her will, in other words. Remember, the original modest insurance had been increased to a hundred thousand dollars. Even after Herbert had got his ten, and the servants perhaps five thousand apiece, there was still eighty thousand left. In other words, the old lady had probably made that will when she had a little capital, and Herbert would get what remained after the legacies. But she'd have to provide for the possibility that he might die before her. Well, she did just that."

"And that's when you left the message for Mr. Glenn?"

"It is. He said that the will was in the bank, and he'd get it in the morning."

He finished his coffee, and then looked at me.

"Here's where you come in," he said. "You'd said that whoever saw to it that Miss Juliet got those doses of strychnia yesterday had to know that they would be fatal only in her condition. That looked like the doctor, didn't it? But I happened to know that Arthur Glenn had recently defended a case where something similar had happened; not the same thing, but he had had to read up on toxicology.

"When I set that trap last night, I knew that it was for one of those two men. I didn't know which, but I knew that the Lenz girl was mixed up in it somehow. She knew Stewart; she used to keep books for him.

And she knew Glenn. And you had revealed something yesterday afternoon, when you were scolding me! You'd told her that Paula had been trying to get upstairs to get a letter. You weren't looking at her then, but I was. She simply blazed.

"You see, everyone in that plot knew that Herbert had left such a letter, or threatened to. Paula and Charlie Elliott weren't the only people who wanted it, and wanted it desperately.

"But something else, too, had happened yesterday afternoon. Paula told Glenn and Stewart that she had married Herbert Wynne. I didn't know that, or I'd have had her watched last night. But whichever one of them was guilty, Paula had to be done away with before she spread that news. Hugo also. When the Lenz girl and Herbert quarreled, it's almost certain that she ceased being the go-between, and Hugo took it over. That is, Hugo gave Herbert the cash for those insurance premiums.

"It's pretty clear that Herbert didn't know who was providing it. He may have suspected, but I doubt if he knew until he had that visitor on Monday night; the man he knew, so that he was not alarmed, the man who smoked the cigar.

"I didn't know myself. I didn't know which of those two men it was until I ran into that third-floor room last night, and found him where you had knocked him senseless with that door."

"And it was . . . ?"

"It was Arthur Glenn," he said soberly. "He'd been in the market, and he was desperate. Desperate all this week, too. Just how desperate you'll know when I tell you that Miss Juliet Mitchell never dictated that

269

statement you signed. The one she dictated never mentioned Charlie Elliott. What she told was that she had known of that newspaper dodge, and had taken the paper and given it to Mary to hide.

"But Glenn had had a warning of what was coming, and so he prepared another statement, one of his own. He shifted them before you went in that day, and she never knew the difference. She had to go, of course, after that. He had taken a tiger by the tail, and he didn't dare to let go. But I don't know yet whether he substituted those tablets himself, or Florence did it."

"She did it," I said with conviction.

He got up and stretched himself.

"Well, I think she did, at that," he said. "One thing's certain: Glenn went to that house late last Monday night to have a showdown with Herbert. More than that, he went there to kill him, if he had to. The chances are that Florence's getting those keys out of Paula's bag was just a bit of luck; but it may have been more. She wasn't in love with Herbert any more, but she might still have been jealous. I haven't a doubt myself that she knew Paula had the keys, and from that to getting them . . .

"Anyhow, Glenn carried a revolver with him that night as well as Paula's keys; and he had that newspaper in his pocket, all ready in case he needed to leave it behind him, bullet hole and all. If there was a verdict of accidental death, he would be sitting pretty. If it was murder, and he was by any chance involved, he could point to that paper and save his life. If it was suicide—well, it was just too bad, and he was out several thousand dollars and the balance

270

when Miss Juliet's angina killed her.

"Well, he left the paper all right. But he didn't need to use his own gun. There was Herbert's, all ready on the bureau. He may still have worn his gloves, or he used a handkerchief. Anyhow, he left no prints on it.

"He had no trouble getting in or getting out. He knew about that sawed-off bolt on the landing door; maybe from Florence. And he moves lightly, for a heavy man.

"But figure up what happened! The old lady gets that alibi of his, and carts it away! And we guess a murder! Moreover, Mary has hidden the paper even from Hugo, and tells him she has burned it! Whatever is coming to him in the next world, Glenn has had his bit of hell already in this. And get this, too! Florence had got Glenn where she wanted him by that time. I doubt if there was anything she didn't either know or guess. She had him chained, and I think he hated her. It's my guess that, if he confesses, he'll involve her, and involve her plenty!"

I suppose I yawned then, for he got up.

"Well, I owe you a lot, Miss Pinkerton. And not the least is a chance to get some sleep."

I yawned again. I could hardly keep my eyes open.

"I want a week of it," I said. "I want a week of sleep, without a break. And I'm ready to start right now."

He smiled at that, and picked up his hat. But he looked at the canary as he moved to the door.

"Dick," he said, "you know your mistress better than I do. But I regard that as a hint. What about you?"

"Don't be foolish," I said sharply. "I meant that I don't want a case for a week."

"I suppose she knows that there is one case she can have for life, Dick," he said. "But she is a hardhearted young woman, and not looking her best just now at that, Dick. Not looking her best."

He turned around and grinned at me.

"Well, I'll run along. Have to see the D. A. and tell him he's been fishing for a minnow and got a whale. And after that I shall buy and *send*—not deliver—a pair of surgical scissors. Well, that's a policeman's life!"

He opened the door, and stopped with his hand on the knob.

"You can let me know when you want to take a case again, little Miss Pinkerton."

"What sort of case?" I asked suspiciously.

"A very long and hard case, involving a life sentence, chains and what have you," he said.

Then he closed the door, and I could hear him whistling softly to himself as he went down the stairs.